A PRAIRIE FIRE?

. . . Martha glanced around wildly: the wheat fields east of the barn were raging with flames and smoke!

"Papa . . . Jake! The wheat's on fire!"

Jake and papa jumped up from eating their lunch and rushed out of the house, grabbing milk pails off of the gateposts as they sped toward the well. She seized the first thing she could find in the lean-to—a battered dishpan—and limped out after them.

By this time papa and Jake were flinging their meager bucketfuls of water on the blazing wheat. Martha hobbled across the yard, angry because she could not run. Soon she was staring helplessly at the once-beautiful wheat stalks, shriveled by the fire and fading from black, to gray, to pale wisps of nothing. . . .

Harvest Gold

Esther Loewen Vogt

Illustrated by
Seymour Fleishman

David C. Cook Publishing Co.

ELGIN, ILLINOIS—WESTON, ONTARIO
FULLERTON, CALIFORNIA

HARVEST GOLD
© 1978 David C. Cook Publishing Co.

Published by David C. Cook Publishing Co., Elgin, IL 60120
Edited by Janet Hoover Thoma

Printed in the United States of America
Library of Congress Catalog Number: 77-87257
ISBN: 0-89191-105-7

CONTENTS

1
SECRETS

MARTHA PULLED HER long gray skirt over her bare legs and sighed. The late May afternoon was warm, and her seat on the stoop of the sod house grew lumpy and uncomfortable. Fromm, the big yellow collie, padded up to her and nosed her knees gently as it scrunched down on its haunches.

"What do you want, Fromm? A big, sad-looking dog like you . . ." She paused, riffling the short hair on his tawny head. She smiled a little, remembering Alice Tinsley's chuckle over Fromm's name. Alice was her best friend who lived down the road.

"What a funny name for a dog! What does it mean?" Alice had asked her.

"Fromm? Oh—it's German for sober or pious. Did you ever see a more solemn-looking dog?"

"Silly! Dogs and cats don't laugh or cry," Alice had replied, and Martha had added, "Sometimes Fromm is happy though. That waggly tail—" The girls had both laughed.

"You want me to come with you?" Martha asked the dog now, watching Fromm's tail thumping beside her.

Or did those sounds come from the barn? For an hour Martha had heard hammering and sawing above the hens' cackle; maybe that was what Fromm begged her to see.

Flipping her wheat-colored braids onto her back, Martha Friesen skipped toward the barn part of the house, her bare toes wiggling in the hard-tamped earth. The grass in the farmyard—once tall like prairie grass—was now close-cropped. Chickens scratched at it, and enough folks walked there that the grass did not grow long as it had in 1877 when the Mennonites moved to Kansas from the Ukraine.

The sound of hammering stopped. Then the *zzzz* of the saw took over as Martha paused in the doorway of the barn. A dim, gaunt shape was kneeling on the hay-covered dirt floor, a hammer in one hand and a piece of board in the other. Papa looked up and raised one bushy eyebrow slightly when he saw her. A wood curl teetered over his ear.

"Martha? Anything you want?" He chattered in the Low German language that the Mennonites still spoke at home.

Martha eyed the box-like structure papa was working on. The boards were nailed together with curved rocker-like pieces on the bottom. It looked like a baby's cradle. But why would papa build a cradle? The Friesens had only eighteen-year-old Jake and herself, and she was now close to eleven.

"Papa—" Martha began lamely, "why are you building a baby's cradle?"

Papa bent over the saw again, and the wood curl fell to the ground. Then the saw sounded sharply as he cut off the too long arc-shape to make the cradle rock smoothly.

"Eh? *Vot* you say, Martha?" he asked.

"That cradle. Who is it for?"

He moistened his thumb with his tongue and rubbed it gently on the cradle's front panel. Then he eyed her strangely, as though he wanted to tell her but did not know how. He placed two nails between his teeth, then took them out again.

"*Ach, ja.* Martha, you are only eleven years old, too young to know." He laid the hammer down and stroked his bearded chin thoughtfully. "But I will tell you, anyhow. Mama ... is going to have a . . . little one."

Martha's dark eyes grew wide. "A baby!" she cried.

He nodded shyly. "In a few months." He picked up his hammer again and drove in another nail, as though he wanted to drown out the words he had just spoken.

Martha jumped up and ran to the barn door. She knew the baby would be a girl: Martha's very own playmate. She looked out over the wide prairie that stretched out to the east like a pale, mauve tablecloth, embroidered with blue primroses, white asters, and spicy pink roses. A stiff breeze blew the fragrance of purple clover into her face, and she breathed deeply. Then she looked across the road to the south, where wheat fields dipped and swelled like a billowing green sea.

To think she would have a baby sister to share this beautiful new land—the Kansas land European Mennonites had settled. She would tell her little sister how it all happened—the way her brother Jake had explained it to her only a year or so ago. How the Mennonites had gone to Russia from Holland, Germany, Switzerland, and other European countries many years ago because they were promised freedom of worship and freedom from serving in the Russian army if they settled the fertile Ukraine Valley. The Mennonites were good farmers. Many had grown rich, which some Russian leaders did not like, so they began to threaten the Mennonites.

And that was when papa and mama and many other Mennonites had left everything and fled to America, settling on the prairie land offered by the Santa Fe railroad. The first settlers had come in the early 1870s. Now it was 1878, and much of the prairie had been sowed with Turkey Red wheat—the hard winter wheat the Mennonites had brought with them.

Martha remembered how Jake had been unhappy in Kansas at first because of the prairie fires, the rattlesnakes, the tornadoes, the heavy winter storms—and an occasional encounter with a friendly Indian like Gray Fox. But the wheat had thrived, and now the millers wanted it because Turkey Red made fine bread. Jake was working for the Danner Mills some seventy miles away. Most Mennonites were still poor, because they had left nearly everything in Russia, so they built cheap sod houses. But there were also good farms in Kansas, belonging to the Americans who had fought in the Civil War.

Now there would be a baby sister to grow up in this new land with her. She could not keep the good news to herself. She whirled around to face papa again.

"Papa, may I run over to visit Alice for an hour? I haven't seen her since school was out a week ago, and we have so much to talk about."

11

"You may go," papa mumbled with his mouth full of nails. "But you must not tell her what I told you . . . about the little one. Such things are not for children to discuss."

The excitement in Martha's eyes dimmed. How could she keep her news from Alice? They shared everything. "I'll try hard not to tell her," she said slowly as she turned to go.

"Wait."

Papa took the nails from his mouth and wiggled his mustache. "I have some more news. We have bought a farm about five miles southeast of here. We plan to move after harvest. You can tell Alice about that."

Move? Away from Alice, from the sod house with its funny grass roof and the young cherry trees and new mulberry grove north of the hen house? Move away from the other Mennonites who lived along the village-like road with farms stretching behind their houses? She shook her head feebly, her braids swinging a little. She did not know whether to be happy or sad.

2
AT YOUR
SERVICE, MA'AM

MARTHA HURRIED TOWARD the house for her sunbonnet. The fresh aroma of baking bread drifted through the open doorway, making her mouth water. But suppertime was still hours away.

Quickly she grabbed her pink bonnet from behind the door and jammed it on her head. Then she turned to look at her mother, who was seated in the creaky walnut rocker, sewing.

"Mama?" Martha said as she crossed the room.

The pretty brown-haired woman hurriedly tucked her sewing under her big gray-and-white checked apron and looked up. "*Ja,* Martha?"

"Papa said I could go to Alice's for an hour. He also told me—" She stopped when she remembered papa's warning. Her face flushed, and she began again, "Papa says we are going to move."

"*Ach, ja.* The farm we are buying is larger than this one. Only by God's grace will we be able to pay for it. Are you happy about moving?"

Martha lowered her eyes. "I will miss my friends here."

"I know you and Gerta Harms haven't played together much."

"Oh, but there's Alice. I'll miss her most of all."

"Maybe." Mama's eyes took on a faraway look that made Martha wonder if she was thinking about the baby. "Well, you had better get over to Tinsleys' if you want to play before chores," she added.

Martha started for the door. Then she turned to look at mama once more. In one glance she saw mama had taken her sewing out from under her apron and held it up—a gray flannel baby gown with a long full skirt and dainty red stitching around the neck. Even babies wore gray if they were Mennonites.

She stepped over Fromm, who drowsed on the threshold, and raced down the driveway, her bare toes curling on earth packed hard by wagon wheels. As she turned onto the road, she caught sight of Gerta Harms's plump figure bent over a garden hoe. *Scritch . . . scritch.* As usual, Gerta was not hurrying.

14

Gerta looked up when Martha reached her. "*Na,* Martha, where are you going this time of day?" she said as she stopped to lean against the hoe. The gravel path, which crept up to her family's A-shaped house, was flanked on each side with beds of purple iris. Gerta seemed to eye the weeds in these beds sleepily. If she got much fatter, Martha was sure the boys would make fun of her.

"I'm going to Alice's for an hour."

"Don't you ever help your mother?" Gerta burst out. "Why, I work all day long. I never have time—"

"My work doesn't take all day," Martha cut in tartly.

"If school weren't out, I would never get done," Gerta went on. She hacked at one dandelion, ignoring the others around it. "You're always spending time with Alice. Don't you ever get tired of playing with English-speaking girls?"

"Alice is my best friend," Martha cried. "After we move, I won't see her much," she added as she started on.

"You're going to move away?" Gerta replied, her voice rising with surprise. "I wonder who will live on your place."

Martha whirled around. "I don't know. Papa didn't say." Then she ran down the road toward the Tinsleys' store. If she stopped any

15

longer, she would not have much time with Alice.

The Tinsleys' store always smelled of drying apples, ground coffee, and pickles that floated in a tart brine in an open barrel. Alice's father was a Civil War veteran, who had opened a store on the land he had bought with his mustering-out pay. Sometimes Alice helped him by sorting the apples and onions to make sure none were rotten.

"Good afternoon, Martha. May I help you?" Mr. Tinsley was weighing sugar from a large gunny sack on the floor.

Martha wished for a penny to buy a few peppermints. But one bought candy for special occasions, and then only if there were money to spare, which was almost never.

"I just wondered if Alice was here," Martha said shyly. "I can play for an hour, if Alice isn't busy."

"Alice is never too busy for her best friend," Mr. Tinsley replied as he tied a brown paper bag with a bit of string. "She's up at the house."

Martha left by the side door and hurried up the cindered path that ran to the back of the frame house. Already the green stalks bordering the path were plump with buds that would soon burst into pink petunias. She knocked lightly.

Alice came to the door, golden-haired and slim in a green full-skirted chambray dress with dainty white rick-rack edging the short puffed sleeves. Her blue eyes sparkled when she saw Martha.

"Oh, Martha! Can you stay to play?" she asked as they went into the kitchen.

Martha always thrilled at the good feel of the cool, blue-checked linoleum against her bare feet and the sight of white muslin curtains stirring at the windows. There were at least five rooms in the Tinsley house, and wallpaper covered the walls. If their new place was half as nice . . .

"For one hour," she answered, glancing at the Seth Thomas clock that ticked loudly on the kitchen shelf.

Alice led Martha into the dining room that held a large glass-paned china cupboard, a round oak table, and cane-bottomed chairs.

"You sit over there in my table-and-chairs set and shut your eyes, Martha."

Alice left the room, and Martha heard the faint, tinkling sound of dishes. She wondered what Alice was doing, but she did not peek.

Finally Alice returned. "All right. You may open your eyes now."

Alice's pink rosebud tea set was on the table—fresh, juicy strawberries in the dishes and a dark sweet drink Alice called cocoa in the tiny cups. A doll whose face looked like a real baby's sat in one of Alice's blue chairs. The doll wore a crocheted bonnet trimmed in blue satin ribbon.

"*Ach*—" Martha gasped. "Why, it looks like a real baby! Oh, Alice, how did you know I'm going to have a baby sister?" Then she clapped her hand over her mouth.

"A baby?" Alice echoed. "How wonderful!"

Martha nodded. "*Ja*. But papa said we were not to discuss it, so let's pretend I never said a word."

"Why, Martha? I think it's the most exciting news I've heard!"

"He said it's not for girls to talk about. But I can tell you my other news."

Alice bit into a strawberry and licked the red juice from her fingers. "What other news? I hope it's as exciting as that."

Martha set her cup down slowly. "Alice, we're moving . . . to another farm five miles away."

"Moving? But you can't do that. You've got to stay."

"No." Martha shook her head staunchly. "We Mennonites do everything by prayer. You know that, Alice. If papa and mama feel it is God's will that we move . . . *ach*, don't you see?"

Alice's blonde head drooped, and her shoul-

18

ders sagged. Then she looked up, her eyes shiny. "Yes, I do see," she said slowly. "But I'll miss you, Martha. If you get a baby sister, you'll have a playmate but not me."

"There's still Gerta. She can be your best friend, Alice."

"Gerta!" Alice spat out the name. "Gerta's too slow and bossy to be my best friend." Alice's blue eyes grew moist.

Martha got up and threw her arms around her friend. After a while Alice blew her nose and said, "Martha, I'm happy for you, I really am. We'll see each other once in a while. It's not as though you're moving back to Russia."

Martha drew back. "*Ach,* I hope we never do that!" she cried. "I like America and Kansas, even if we are poor."

"Some day the Mennonites will be important, too. And I'll always remember my dearest friend was a Mennonite girl," Alice replied.

Martha nodded. Alice was right. Picking up the tiny tea cup, she asked, "Our party isn't over, is it? I'd like more co-coca, please."

Alice giggled at Martha's pronunciation. Although Martha's English had improved, she still spoke with a German accent. Then Alice poured the brown liquid into Martha's cup. "At your service, ma'am. At your service."

3
THRESHING
AND PACKING

MARTHA HUNG THE JUST-WASHED APRONS and shirts on the clothesline east of their house. As she reached into the clothes basket for more, she looked around to see a familiar figure walking up the driveway.

She threw the clothespins she was holding on the ground and raced to meet her brother. "Jake!" she shrieked. "Oh, Jake, you're home!"

He grabbed her and spun her around. "Martha, you are getting to be a big girl. Why, I hardly knew you just now—hanging up clothes like a real farmer's daughter."

She wriggled herself free. "Mama needs my help like papa needs yours. Does Mr. Danner mind if you help with the harvest?"

"Not if he gets our wheat for his mills. Is it ready to cut?"

"Papa's in the field right now. Just think, we don't need the scythes this year. We have a reaper to cut it."

"Oh, yes, the one papa bought from Tinsley, after he bought a harvester with a self-binder."

"Things get easier all the time. Just think, with a self-binder farmers don't have to tie the sheaves together!" Martha exclaimed.

"That's just like the mills," Jake added. "Danner's thinking of converting from water power to steam."

They had reached the house, and Martha opened the door. Mama was stirring in a large black pot on the stove. As she turned, a happy look crossed her face. "Jacob, you came!"

"It's good to be home, mama," he replied, throwing his big arms around her.

"How did you come?" mama said as she went back to her cooking.

"I walked a part of the way. Then Ben Nickel came along with a wagonload of lumber and brought me the rest of the way." He paused and sniffed hungrily. "Say, something smells good. What are you cooking?"

"Parsnip soup made with beef. And we'll have butter and fresh bread. Better get washed up; papa will be in soon."

During dinner, Jake told them about his job, speaking mostly English but lapsing back into Low German now and then. Soon he wanted to know about the farm. "How do you like the new reaper?"

"*Ach,* it cuts everything so fast! We will be done in a few days." Papa was already up and out of the door.

"After the harvest and threshing is done, I'll stay to help you move. Have you seen the new place, Martha?" Jake asked as he pushed away from the table to join papa in the fields.

Martha shook her head. "I hope the house will have a real floor, not dirt like this one."

Jake laughed. "You will be surprised, I think—pleasantly so."

Martha wasn't sure what the word *pleasantly* meant, but it sounded good. She cleared the dishes from the table and plunged them into sudsy water in the big tin dishpan. The mid-June air was still and hot, and sweat dampened her forehead. The heavy swirl of chaff, straw, and dust hung around her. She could hear the faint, whirring sounds of the reaper as it cut swathes of wheat and the snorts of horses as they pranced through the stubble.

Last year papa and Mr. Enns had harvested the wheat with scythes and sickles. But now the machine cut the wheat with its tiny, sharp knives. Jake would walk behind to tie the wheat into sheaves and set them up into shocks. Yes, harvest ought to go faster this year.

In another week or so, they would leave this

22

sod house, and she would see very little of Alice. But at least Jake was here—Jake, who loved fun and laughter.

As the hot days wore on, the horse-drawn thresher rumbled into the yard and onto the field, where it blew a stack of fresh straw beyond the pasture. Then Jake hauled wagon-loads of wheat to the railroad station, where it was loaded into cars and shipped to Danner's Mills.

When the last bundle had been gobbled up by the thresher's maw and the golden kernels stopped pouring from its spout, Martha knew the time to move had come. For several days she had helped mama stack featherbeds and pillows into piles and wrap their best dishes between layers of quilts. The pictures of Grandpa and Grandma Hiebert had been taken down from the shelf and tucked into the tray of the big ironbound trunk, together with her brown velvet bonnet and other clothes.

Outside, papa and Jake, Mr. Enns, and several other neighbors, who had come with their wagons, were tying washtubs, rakes, shovels, and coops of squawking chickens onto three wagons. Then they stomped into the house and carried out the sturdy, handmade table and benches, the walnut rocker, other pieces of furniture, and the new cradle. They piled them in every bit of space that remained.

Jake stole up behind Martha and tweaked her ear. "Got everything, little sister? Your pink sunbonnet?"

"You think I'd forget that, Jake?" she flared. "The old gray babushkas we used to wear I would gladly leave behind, but not my very own bonnet."

"How about your smile? Seems to me I haven't seen it for days. What's the matter, Martha?"

"It's Alice," she gulped. "What if we never see each other again?"

"*Hui,* do you think we're moving to the moon?" he scoffed. "Of course, you'll see Alice."

Martha's eyes crinkled into laughter as she thought of Jake's funny words. As if anybody would ever reach the moon!

Papa tossed Martha over the wheel onto the wagon seat, then carefully lifted mama up beside her. Mama looked tired. No wonder. These had been busy weeks—first the harvesting and threshing, then the packing and getting ready to move.

As the wagons creaked down the driveway, with Fromm trotting behind the last one, Martha turned to say good-bye to their sod house. She remembered leaving the village of Pastwa in the Ukraine, riding in borrowed wagons until they reached the railroad sta-

Martha darted into the new house.

tion. That had been hard because she knew she would never see their village again. But now she promised herself, *I'll come back here. And soon I'll have a baby sister.*

Still, leaving did make her feel sad. She hardly saw the fields and farms, the groves of hackberry and mulberry trees bordering the narrow dirt road that led to their new house five miles away.

The ride did not take long. Martha began to look for the new house when papa said they were still a half mile away. Soon Jake, riding on the wagon in front of her, pointed to the east side of the road. Up ahead Martha saw the gray roof of a barn and several smaller buildings. Hidden in a circle of half-grown trees stood a white frame house like the Tinsleys', not a crumbling pile of sod or adobe bricks.

Martha could hardly wait until they pulled into the yard. Finally the horses turned, and the wagon clanked up the drive. She could see a square house now with shutters to keep out the hot sun. Several elm and cottonwood trees threw a lacy shadow on the hard-packed earth around the house that was enclosed by a white picket fence.

As soon as papa shouted "Whoa!" Martha slid over the wagon wheel and darted through the open gate and into the door of the lean-to that stood at the side of the house. Her bare feet felt cool against the scrubbed board floor. She ran from room to room—four of them besides the lean-to. The walls and woodwork in three rooms were painted a drab gray, but one room had faded, blue-flowered wallpaper. It was beautiful!

Martha could scarcely wait until the furniture was brought in, even though there would only be a few pieces for each room.

"Bring Martha's bed into the little back room," mama called out as she carried in a bundle of quilts. Then she turned to Martha. "You see? You will have a room all to yourself. The room with the wallpaper will be the parlor, and papa and I will sleep in the other back room. This room here in front will be the dining room, where we'll eat if there's company. We will cook in the lean-to. How do you like that?"

"Oh, mama! That's marvelous!" she cried, trying out a new English word. "I didn't know we would have such a fine house. It's almost as nice as the Tinsleys'!"

Just then, Jake entered. After setting the walnut rocker down, he flipped her pink sunbonnet back. "And that isn't all. South of the barn there's a grove of trees—like a little woods. I'll bet you'll like it."

Martha ran out of the house. Sure enough,

behind the weatherbeaten barn was a wooded area. She tiptoed carefully through the weeds and nettles to find a cool, quiet place. The trees had grown tall and shady, and Martha knew it would be a comfortable place to play.

Suddenly she spied a fenced-off area just beyond the woods near the road. Some tombstones jutted over the weeds and high grass, while others lay on top of the hard, weed-grown mounds. A cemetery, right on the corner of their farm! But who lay buried there? Mennonites had lived here only a few years, and Martha knew they had used another cemetery.

She found a loose board in the fence and crawled through. Then she knelt down, crushing the dry grass as she read: *Elias Dobbs, born 1807, died 1863 . . . Mary Durbin, beloved wife of Samuel Durbin, born 1812, died 1868 Thy will be done.* And many more. Why, these were not Mennonites. They were people who had lived here during the Civil War, people like the Tinsleys. The place looked deserted and lonely.

"I'll be back," Martha said aloud as she crept back through the fence. These pitiful graves looked like they needed someone to care for them.

FRIENDLY NEIGHBORS?

THE LEAN-TO SMELLED OF SPICES and brine and the pungent odor of dill and hot vinegar. Martha had just finished the dinner dishes and hung the dish pan on a nail on the wall.

"Martha," mama said, holding out a tin cup. "I want you to go across the road and borrow a cup of vinegar from Mrs. Petker. I need just a bit more so I can finish putting up these pickles."

"But mama, I don't know the Petkers. I won't know what to talk about."

"*Eeeee,* then it is high time you do. We are Mennonites, and so are they. It is only neighborly to borrow from each other."

If we hadn't moved, Martha thought, *I might have gone to Tinsley's store, and Alice and I could have chatted for a few minutes.*

"Better tie a clean apron over your dress,"

mama added, eyeing Martha's brown chambray. "Your dress is none too clean."

Martha opened the chimney cupboard in her room and took out a fresh apron. She shook out the crisply starched folds and tied the narrow bands around her waist. Then she came back to the lean-to for her pink sunbonnet and the cup. As she slammed out of the house and started for the gate, Fromm nudged her gently.

"Coming with me?" she asked him.

He gave a friendly whimper and followed her down the rutted lane. The morning sun was already warm, and the dry ground felt hot beneath her bare feet. She crossed the road and hurried up the Petkers' driveway with the collie at her heels.

The George Petker farm consisted of a ramshackle two-room frame house, a stone barn, and several tired-looking outbuildings, propped up by hedge posts.

As Martha came into the yard, three boys wearing faded blue shirts and dun-colored trousers rushed up to meet her.

" 'Morning," the largest one called out. He looked about fifteen years old. "And who do you be?"

"My name's Martha Friesen. We moved in across the road three days ago. Who are you?"

"*Hui,* you're the new neighbor." The boy

30

grinned and pointed to himself. "I'm Eli. Them other two are Sam and Fred. We got a big brother Abram and baby Solly."

"You got any brothers?" Sam asked, staring at her hard.

She felt uncomfortable. "Just Jake. He came home to help with the harvest, but he'll go back to work in the mills soon."

She wiggled her foot in the dirt as she looked them over. Sam seemed about her age—eleven or so. Fred was probably seven. There were no girls.

"*Ach,* we had hoped you would be a boy," Fred grouched. He turned away. "Might as well finish my mud fort."

"What's the cup for?" Eli asked. He had moved in front of Martha, his hands on his hips.

"Mama wants to borrow some vinegar."

"Vinegar!" Sam hooted with laughter. "Does she think ma is as sour as that?"

Martha's face reddened, and Sam laughed again.

"Mama is putting up cucumber pickles, and borrowing is neighborly," she said in a soft voice.

Eli frowned. "As if we have anything worth borrowing. . . . We may have some grape vinegar in the cave. Last summer we picked wild grapes from the creek, and pa made them into

31

wine—except that it turned to vinegar."

"Eli!" Sam growled. "Pa will tan your hide for telling about the wine. If Elder Wiens hears about this—"

"Who cares?" Eli muttered. "It's all the vinegar we have."

"*Ach,* I don't know." Martha hesitated. Mama had not mentioned grape vinegar, for she believed in good vinegar made from apple cider. But mama always said one could not be choosy. "Well, I guess grape vinegar will do."

She started for the shack, but just then, a lanky figure barreled from behind the house, a huge black dog after him. The hair on Fromm's neck rose, and he let out a low growl.

"Down, Fromm," she cautioned. He nosed her skirt and obediently squatted on his haunches. The tall boy marched toward her. Then he reached out and jerked the pink sunbonnet over her eyes.

"I see it's our charming new neighbor. But I can't see your face. Mennonite girls shouldn't wear sunbonnets. They should stick with babushkas. . . . What's your name?"

Martha shrank back a little. Adjusting her bonnet, she bit her lower lip sharply.

"I'm—Martha. Who're you?"

He threw his head back and laughed. "I thought Mennonite girls were supposed to be shy and polite. Well, I'm Abram, and I'm twenty years old. Surprised?" His gaze mocked her.

Her cheeks turned pink as she started toward the house, her dog following. Abram blocked her way.

"Now wait a minute, Martha," he said boldly. "You needn't rush off in a huff. I won't bite." He laughed again.

Fromm growled some more, and Abram whirled on the dog. "Better keep your mutt away from Cinder, else you'll be sorry. Cinder would gladly chew him into sausage."

Martha put one hand on Fromm's head, forcing him down. "Down, Fromm," she ordered out loud. "Some people need to polish their manners," she added as she tried to go around the young man who acted like a child.

Abram grabbed her arm roughly. "Now just a minute. I didn't mean anything bad, so you'd better sweeten up. I like to be neighborly as well as anyone."

Fromm jerked away and bared his teeth, but dropped his tail when Martha commanded him. With a snarl, Cinder flew at Fromm, ready to fight.

"Call your dog off!" Martha shouted. "Fromm will kill him!"

Abram laughed scornfully. "Let's see him try. That runt can't hurt a fly, much less Cinder!"

The three boys laughed as the two dogs ogled each other.

"Call off your dog, Abram!" Martha cried again, frightened by the dog's loud barking and bared teeth.

The unkempt boy grabbed his straw hat from his head and waved it wildly. "Sic 'em, Cinder!" he yelled.

With a bound the big dog caught Fromm by the throat and tossed him like a rag doll. Then he sprang for him again. Fromm seemed helpless against the mongrel's fury. Martha watched, frozen silent.

Eli chuckled, and Abram was bent over laughing. "Kill Cinder, will he?" he shouted shrilly. "It's the other way around!"

Fromm's tan coat was bloody by this time, and Martha shivered with fear.

Suddenly Fromm shook himself and leaped on Cinder with a growl of anger. Cinder yelped with pain. Fromm caught him by the throat, close behind the jaws, and hung on. The black dog shook and growled and shook again. He thrashed madly and swung and twisted and howled, but he could not free himself. Then he stopped shaking and began to pant. Now Fromm rattled the big dog without losing his hold until Cinder gasped.

"You call your dog off!" Abram yelled hoarsely, his face pasty-white. Martha stood stunned; the words of command stuck in her throat.

Just then Sam rushed on the two dogs, beating them as he tried to tear them apart. What if the dogs attacked him? Martha's throat muscles loosened.

"Fromm, come here!" she screamed. "You should be ashamed of yourself."

The tawny collie slowly let go of Cinder, a shamed look on his face.

The three boys watched silently. Then Sam turned to Martha. "You have a good dog."

She patted Fromm's blood-streaked head. "He's all right—for a dog. I hope he didn't hurt Cinder."

Cinder had slunk away and was crawling under the house. Eli grinned. *"Hui,* he'll live. But if Abram hadn't sicced him—"

"Your ma will be wanting her vinegar," Abram cut in sharply as he stalked away.

Martha's legs shook as she started for the door of the shack. Sam caught up with her. He looked friendly.

"Sorry, Martha. It wasn't your fault. I hope we can still be neighbors. Some time we'll take you fishing with us."

"Ach, ja," she said breathlessly. "We can still be neighbors."

5

A LAND OF STRANGERS

MARTHA STOOD BY the north window of her bedroom and looked at the dull, brown landscape. For days the blistering July wind had blown across the prairies, scorching the leaves of the young cottonwoods until they drooped limp and lifeless.

"*Ach,* it's too hot to go to church," she muttered. But she knew it made no difference. Papa would say, "On the seventh day God rested from his labors," and so would they—in church. Even the wind had stopped blowing, as though it wanted a rest.

She tugged the long, dark blue skirt over her head and fastened the hooks and eyes carefully. Her hair was already combed back, smooth and taut, and braided into two thick ropes that fell down her back.

Picking up a fresh three-cornered scarf, she started for the dining room.

"Ready to go, Martha?" Jake asked as he came from the parlor to get papa's big German Bible from the corner table in the dining room.

Martha headed for the lean-to, then paused. "Mama isn't quite ready. Jake, I know we're going to another church because papa says it's closer and needs our help. But will it be another sod building like the old one?"

"*Hui,* why would we need that? This church is in Warren schoolhouse. You'll go to school there in the fall."

"But I won't know anyone at this church," she wailed.

"Soon you will. Besides, our neighbors the Petkers will be there."

"*Ach,* them!" Martha made a wry face. Mama had not been happy with the grape vinegar. "Five ornery boys. Who needs that?"

Jake laughed. "Well, at least, we don't live in a dull neighborhood with Gerta Harms!"

Just then mama came out of the bedroom. Her face seemed tired; gray lines crisscrossed her fine, high forehead. She placed her hands on Martha's shoulders and eyed her dully.

"Did you wash your neck and ears good?" she asked.

Martha nodded.

Then mama started toward the lean-to door, and Martha followed. The hot sun beat down on the wagon and horses tied to the hitching post near the gate. Jake hoisted her over the wagon wheel. Papa had placed straw on the floor so Martha could spread her skirt out like a fan. After mama was seated on the wooden seat, papa clucked, and the team moved slowly down the lane.

Martha watched the farms, scattered on either side of the road, as the wagon clanked and thumped along. The air lay like a thick band around them. Even the brown sparrows twittering along the fences seemed to be scolding the hot day.

Buggies and wagons were already parked along the hitching row when they reached the schoolyard. The horses were stomping and snorting at the flies that bit their heels. Papa pulled in front of the door to unload.

The wooden building felt cool when Martha entered. She waited in the dim hall for papa, mama, and Jake. Then she and mama sat on the right side of the room with the womenfolk, papa and Jake on the left with the men. There were crude wooden benches—some with flat tablelike pieces over the top for schoolwork.

Martha glanced around at the schoolroom, which was already filling with people. She knew only a few. Her old friends, like Gerta and birdlike Amelia Funk, weren't there. They attended church in the old immigrant building, where everyone spoke the Low German dialect and the minister preached in pure German.

Here a pert, brown-eyed girl wearing a clever Dutch bonnet sat next to the open window. And a plump taffy-haired girl scrunched behind her, staring insolently at every newcomer.

Across the room she saw the row of Petker boys. Eli saw her looking at them and winked slyly. She turned away quickly.

There were other children, but they all looked alike. Besides, they were strangers. She could not see anyone she would like to be friends with.

After everyone was settled, the service began. First they rose to sing *Groszer Gott, Wir Loben Dich* ("Holy God, We Praise Thy Name"). Then Elder Wiens ambled to the front. He read the text from a big German Bible, squinting as he moved one finger along word by word: "That the Lord thy God may show us the way wherein we may walk, and the thing we may do."

His sermon was long, intoned in a deep sonorous voice. Martha tried to stay awake by watching a gnat buzz over George Petker's fat, bald head. But she almost laughed out loud. Then she sobered quickly. Church was a serious place; to laugh was almost sinful.

The room grew stifling. Men wiped perspiration from their faces with gray handkerchiefs. Martha looked for a piece of paper to fan herself with, but there was nothing.

Something Elder Wiens just said startled her: "God's way is best! Sometimes we want to go our way, but God wants to show us the way."

Martha sat up and blinked. If that were so, God had meant for them to move and would surely give her some friends in this church.

Finally the service was over, and the taffy-haired girl was coming toward her. Martha saw that her plump cheeks were rosy and her eyes a deep blue.

"My name is Liesbet Wiens. Elder Wiens is my father," the girl said, her eyes crinkling into a smile at the corners. "I'm glad you came. Welcome to church!"

Martha nodded and smiled a little. Liesbet's tone sounded like an elder's rather than a friend's. She would probably be bossy like Gerta Harms.

With a sigh, Martha stretched out her hand. "I hope we can be friends, Liesbet." Then she glanced anxiously at mama, who moved slowly toward the door, her face chalk-white. Martha laid a hand on Liesbet's arm. "I have

40

to go and find my papa. Mama doesn't look well."

She hurried through the crowd and found papa talking to a tall, thin man about the price of wheat.

". . . I tell you, if you would raise more wheat—" papa was saying until he noticed Martha's anxious face. "Anything wrong, child?"

"It's mama," Martha whispered. "She looks awfully sick."

The ride home was quiet but endless. Mama leaned heavily against papa's shoulder as Jake hurried the team down the road. The hot wind seared their faces, making Martha wish for her pink sunbonnet. Finally they were home.

Papa helped mama into the bedroom and then came back into the dining room.

"You will have to fix the dinner, Martha. Mama is feeling bad. But change your dress first. You know you must keep your Sunday clothes clean."

Martha had never fixed a meal by herself, but she would try. She took down the smoked ham that dangled from the lean-to ceiling and sliced several thick slabs to fry. Yesterday Mama had made plenty of *pluma moos,* a prune-and-raisin pudding. And there was fresh bread. In the "fraidy cave" (mama's

41

name for the storm cellar) there was the thick butter that mama had churned only a day or so ago.

She wondered about Liesbet, the pert girl with the Dutch bonnet, and the Petker boys. School would never be the same without Alice. And mama would need Martha's help after the new baby came.

I know what I'll do, Martha decided as she turned the ham slices in the big iron skillet. *I'll stay home from school and help mama. It will be easier than learning to know a lot of strangers.*

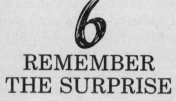

6
REMEMBER
THE SURPRISE

MARTHA WAS AWAKENED from a heavy sleep by a hand on her shoulder and papa's voice.

"Martha? Martha, wake up!"

Through the open window, she could see stars winking in the black sky. Why should papa wake her in the middle of the night?

"It is time," he said simply. "Get dressed. Jake will drive you to Peter Klassen's, and later I will bring you home again." He lit the lamp and left.

With the smell of burnt match and kerosene drifting over the hot room, Martha rolled out of bed. She fumbled for her clothes and pulled on the drab brown chambray. It was hard to close the hooks and eyes in the dim light. By the time she picked up her comb, papa was rapping on the door impatiently.

"Aren't you coming? You can comb your hair later."

She shuffled into the dimly lit dining room. Eerie shadows danced on the gray walls like spooky elves, and she shivered a little. Jake sat in the walnut rocker, stifling a yawn with the back of his hand. Papa said something to him about Mrs. Eckert, and Jake nodded. Then papa went into mama's bedroom.

"Ready?" Jake said to Martha as he picked up the lighted lantern on the table. She followed him out into the night, watching the swinging yellow arc chase shadows from the humpy lilac bushes. Martha sighed as Jake lifted her over the wagon wheel and onto the wooden seat. After he swung up beside her, he clucked to the horses.

"Giddy-ap . . . git!"

The horses clopped slowly down the lane and turned onto the road. The heat of yesterday had cooled to night softness, and the air was hushed and still. Here and there a frog croaked a *ribbet-ribbet* sound, and once Martha thought she heard an owl hoot in the woods behind the barn.

As the wagon clanked down the road, she swayed drowsily with its rhythm. In the distance she heard a coyote howl—a sound that still frightened her.

Now that she was wide awake, she remembered who Mrs. Eckert was. She was the local midwife who came when babies were born. Would the baby sister be there when she returned? Why did she have to miss all the excitement?

Soon the wagon creaked up Peter Klassen's driveway. When the dogs barked at their arrival, a pinpoint of light flickered inside the farmhouse.

Jake jumped from the wagon and hurried to the door. He spoke a few quick words to Peter, who stood in the kitchen doorway in his long nightshirt, holding a lighted lamp in his hand.

"Come, Martha," Jake called as he returned to the wagon. "Someone will come for you after a while. Chin up, and remember the surprise!"

Mrs. Klassen, hastily dressed in a rumpled, gray-figured dress, met Martha in the kitchen and led her to a wooden settee in the parlor. She piled featherbeds and quilts to make it soft.

"Why not lie down and sleep until morning? It won't be long until daylight, so keep your dress on," she said kindly.

The pillow was fluffy and plump with goose feathers. Martha lay down and closed her eyes after the woman had left the room. But sleep would not come. She was glad her tiny room at home was large enough to hold a cradle. She would clear a shelf in her chimney closet for the baby's clothes. The school papers she had saved from Clear Ridge could be thrown away, and her slate packed in the trunk. Since she would not be going to school in the fall, she did not need them.

Papa had said the baby would be born in a few months, and now it was late July. Outside the birds began to sing, and she knew morning would soon be here. Finally, her eyelids drooped heavier and heavier, and she fell asleep.

When she awoke, the sunshine streamed into the room. She blinked, wondering where she was for a moment. Then she prepared to get up.

Her dress was rumpled; sleeping in starched cotton wrinkled everything. Mama was not here to braid her hair, so she tied it back with a bit of brown yarn she found on the floor. Then she retied her sash and went into the kitchen. Mrs. Klassen was trying to feed a little boy in a high chair. He banged on his table and spit his oatmeal out.

"Hansie!" she said sternly. "If you don't eat now, you will have to go hungry for a while."

"Wah!" he cried, twisting his chubby hands into sticky little fists.

Martha tousled his dark hair. "If you don't want your breakfast, I'll eat it!"

He stared at her curiously, then began to laugh. "Mama . . . Eat . . . eat!" he yelled; then made Martha feed him the rest of the oatmeal.

Mrs. Klassen watched them, an amused smile on her face.

"*Na*, Martha, I guess you will be just what your mama needs."

After breakfast she helped Mrs. Klassen with the dishes, then she went outside and sat on the east side of the house, playing with two gray kittens. They rolled over and over, scratching her bare legs. How long until papa would come for her? A shy little blonde girl peered around the corner of the house, and Martha remembered there was an older child named Eva. She picked up a yellow kitten and brought it to Martha.

Then the dogs began to bark, and Martha jumped up to meet the familiar wagon that rolled up the long driveway. When her father stopped the team, he ignored her excited questions and went inside to talk to Mrs. Klassen. Martha waited on the porch. Why did papa look so grim? Was something wrong?

When he came out, she rushed to him. "*Ach*, papa, are you ready to take me home now?"

He paused and nodded. "*Ja*, we will go home now. Martha—" he began, and she noticed a muscle twitch under his eye. "Martha, you have a baby brother. . . ."

"A brother!" she cried. "How wonderful! I had hoped for a sister, but a brother will do just fine. What's his name, papa?"

Papa swallowed. "We decided to call him Franz. But—"

"But what?"

"Baby Franz is very sick. We—don't know if he will live."

"But he must!" Martha cried. "He can't be sick. When we moved, I had to leave Alice. But it was easier when I knew I would have a baby to play with."

"Whatever God wills, we must accept, Martha," Papa said in a low voice. "Let's drive home now."

Martha sat silently beside him. Her throat felt dry, and she could not speak. She had looked forward to the baby for so long. Now they were not sure he would live.

Dear Jesus, she prayed silently, *Please make Baby Franz well.*

7
BABY FRANZ

WHEN THE WAGON rolled into the lane and pulled to a stop, Martha hopped over the wheel and ran through the gate. As she started for the house, a firm hand stopped her at the lean-to door. It was Mrs. Petker.

"You had better stay outside, Martha."

"But I want to see my baby brother!" she cried, trying to push her way in. Mrs. Petker blocked her path.

"No, you can't do that."

Martha looked sharply at the fat, pie-faced woman. "Why not? Why can't I see him?"

Mrs. Petker gestured helplessly with her hands. "*Ach, ja,* but you cannot go in—just yet."

"Can I see mama then?" she pleaded. "I'll be very quiet."

The bulky woman hesitated. "After a while.

Why don't you play outside now? We'll tell you when you can come in."

Martha walked away slowly. She flopped down on the browning grass under the cottonwoods. Fromm came and touched his wet nose against her arm, and she stroked his tawny head.

"Nobody wants us around, Fromm. Not mama, not papa. Not anyone!"

As she sat there, wagons and buggies creaked up and down the lane, and solemn-faced women went in and out of the house. Some brought loaves of fresh bread covered by tea towels. Others carried large kettles of soup, as though they were feeding a crowd. Martha cowered under the tree, wondering why no one spoke to her. The sun was warm. She had gone off during the night without her pink bonnet, and now she needed it. Twice she had tried to steal into the house to get her bonnet, but she was firmly, yet kindly, pushed back outside. She would try one more time.

But when she opened the lean-to door, a voice said, "Please calm yourself, Martha. It is better if you don't come in just yet."

"But I don't understand . . ." she began, tears lurking in her eyes.

Mrs. Petker shoved a crusty roll into her hand. "Here, eat a bite. Then go and play until we call you."

Martha stared at the roll. She was not hungry. All she wanted was to see Baby Franz, or at least mama.

She wandered slowly through the gate and across the yard. The sun beat hot on the ground and scorched the bottoms of her bare feet. Tiny puffs of dust stirred as she shuffled toward the barn, Fromm trotting behind her. She wondered where Jake was. Then she saw him head slowly toward the cornfield, carrying a hoe. He probably knew no more than she did.

She let herself through the fence behind the barn and started toward the woods, skirting a patch of thistles that grew along the narrow path. The hens were cackling as they scratched in the straw behind the hen house. Martha hopped over a fallen log and looked for a patch of green grass in the cool wooded area. She noticed a gray stump—crumbling into splinters—that looked like an ugly wart in the sun-freckled woods, and she dropped down with a sigh. Burying her head in her arms, she began to cry—softly at first, then in big, gulping sobs. If only Alice Tinsley were near by, she would have someone to talk to.

Suddenly she heard the rumble of horses' hooves behind her, and she turned around. A mangy brown mare clopped along the edge of the tiny cemetery with Abram Petker hunched over its sway back. He swept off his hat and bowed.

"It's the vinegar girl," he said with a harsh laugh. "Tell me why you are drowning the trees."

She stopped crying and looked at him. "Drowning?"

"Well, crying then. I thought you'd be happy because your stupid dog whipped Cinder the other day. Now the way you're carrying on—"

She made a wry face. "I just got a new baby brother, and papa says he's very sick. Nobody lets me in the house or tells me what is happening."

"*Tch, tch,* too bad," he mumbled, jamming his straw hat back over his dark head. "If we'd all stayed in Russia where we belonged, we would have had the finest doctors instead of midwives. But here—" He shrugged his narrow shoulders.

"I like this land," Martha said stubbornly. "It's going to be a good place some day. Our wheat fields are growing like—"

"Like harvest gold."

"Why—yes, that's exactly what they are!" Martha exclaimed. "I believe what papa says: God led us here."

"God!" Abram spat out the word. "He could've taken care of us in Russia, too. We

Mennonites had a good life there. Why, I remember the time Count Tolstoy visited our village."

"I saw the president last year," Martha interrupted. "I went with the Tinsleys to Topeka when President and Mrs. Rutherford B. Hayes were there. And when Willy Tinsley cried, the president spoke—"

"It's not the same!" Abram snorted. "Remember one thing! You'd better do as the government says, or we'll be shipped back to Russia."

"But this is a free land," Martha protested.

"Why do we have English teachers in our schools instead of Mennonite teachers, like we had in Russia?" Abram asked. "Besides, this country doesn't want the Mennonites to become strong."

"Why not?"

"Always want to know everything, don't you?" he growled. "Because . . . that's why!"

"But I'm still glad we're here," she persisted in a softer voice. "Even Jake agrees."

"*Hui,* that's because he's got that good job with the miller. No wonder he changed his tune."

Martha shook her head firmly.

But Abram was not watching. He kicked the mare's thin ribs with his patched boot and rode away.

Abram sure was strange, Martha thought as she shook out her full skirt and started back toward the house. Were there really better doctors in Russia? Martha hoped the news would be good when she asked again.

Reaching the barn, she watched papa come out of the lean-to door and walk slowly toward her. His face did not show any emotion.

Then he placed one arm around her shoulder. "Martha, Baby Franz—" He choked a little now. "Baby Franz has left us to be with Jesus."

Her brown eyes widened. She could not believe it. Where was God when she needed him? Was Abram right? Could God also have cared for them better in Russia?

That night, when Martha stretched out on her bed, she could not pray. It was as though God had brought them to America, and then walked off and forgot them.

8

A NEW LITTLE GRAVE

MARTHA SAT UNDER the big cottonwood tree, her chin cupped in her hands. For an hour she had watched the dull clouds, now heavy with a coming storm, hover low over the trees. The air had been warm and sullen. Then suddenly the wind rose and shifted as it *sssss'd* in the leafy cover above her. She ran into the house just as the first raindrops flicked into her face.

Big, single drops splashed against the windowpane. Then all at once sheets of rain streamed noisily onto the fragrant camomile bed below the window.

As drum rolls of thunder grumbled among the clouds, Martha stood at the west parlor window, thinking of the tiny new grave in the cemetery just beyond the woods. It did not seem possible that only a few days ago they had dressed Baby Franz in the long, flowing white dress with wide lacy bands. He had looked like a delicate wax doll, sleeping in a softly lined box. Even now she could hear the sad voices singing about going home as they marched to the little grave.

She had stolen away to the barn when the coffin was carefully lowered into the deep black hole. After she was safe in the hayloft, she had cried for the baby who should have been sleeping in the new cradle.

Now she wondered what their friends had meant when they sung about going home. Did they mean we would be returning to Russia? she asked herself. Even Abram had said they could stay if they obeyed the government.

Jake came up behind her and tweaked one tightly woven braid. He smelled of leather and horses, for he had been mending harness in the barn.

"Anything wrong, little sister?" he asked as she turned to face him.

She knew her eyes were red but she could not explain her fears to him. A year ago he would have been ready to go back to Russia, since he had not wanted to come here. For a while he had been unhappy and sullen. But now he had come to love the prairies and his job at the mill.

She traced her finger along the wet windowsill. "Will you be leaving to work for Mr.

Danner again?" she asked finally.

"On Friday," he replied. "With this rain, papa won't have work for me here. Mr. Tinsley says papa can use his hoe drill to sow the wheat, so he won't have to broadcast it by hand. Anyway, Mr. Danner needs me. . . . But that isn't why you were crying, is it?"

Martha shook her head. "You will come back sometimes, won't you? I get so lonely. . . ." She tried to hold her tears back.

"Now look here, Martha," he said firmly. "There are girls your age in church. You'll soon make friends."

"I think Liesbet Wiens is going to be bossy like Gerta Harms. And that Annie Isaac is sure to be stuck-up, wearing a Dutch bonnet."

"Well, the Petker boys then. I wouldn't be surprised if they could be fun."

"*Ach,* Jake—them! I can't understand why Baby Franz had to—die. He would have been such fun. I could have helped mama with him and—"

"You can still help mama," Jake reminded her. "She will be in bed for almost another week. Some of the church ladies will help, of course, but you are old enough to fix a good meal like last Sunday."

Was it only last Sunday that she had cooked dinner for the family? She looked at the ticking mantel clock: it was almost noon. She knew there was a kettle of green bean soup, which one of the church people had brought only yesterday.

Tying a clean apron around her waist, she went into the kitchen. She shook the grate of the big black cookstove, stirred the smoldering ashes, and added a few dried chips. Soon the fire blazed merrily, so she pushed the kettle of soup to the front burner. There was plenty of rye bread and butter, too.

Papa came in from the barn a few minutes later. He hung his cap on the nail behind the lean-to door, sniffing hungrily.

"*Na*, Martha, the soup smells good. You are such a big help already."

"But I didn't make it, papa," she replied.

He pulled a chair out and sat down. "Maybe not. But we need you to set the table and wash dishes." He looked at her sharply. "Why so sad, little daughter?"

She lowered her head. "I'm still upset about Baby Franz, papa."

"We must not question God's ways, Martha. We must trust him, not ask foolish questions."

After dinner Martha washed the dishes and hung the dishpan away. The rain had stopped, and the clouds were broken by splinters of sunlight, surrounding the freshly washed earth with a golden haze.

She walked across the wet yard, the mud

Martha stood looking at the tiny grave.

squishing between her bare toes as she wondered if the little grave had washed away. *I'll walk out there and see,* she decided.

Carefully, she crossed the rocky path that led to the woods, her apron wadding between her legs every so often. The tiny mound was still there heaped with prairie flowers that had been bruised and battered by the weather.

She stood looking at the place where her baby brother was buried until Abram Petker rode up again. "*Hui,* and what are you doing here in this valley of bones?" he asked in his mocking way.

"I just came to see—" she paused, not wanting to cry in front of someone who was always taunting her.

"The little grave where they buried your baby brother?" Abram finished for her. "I'm sorry, Martha. I really am."

He seemed almost kind today, so she continued on. "It's hard to understand. Papa says Baby Franz is in heaven, and so did Elder Wiens."

"There's no way a tiny babe can get out of a grave and fly up to heaven! Don't you see?" He whirled around and rode away.

Martha started toward the house more bewildered than ever. Was Abram right? How could Baby Franz be in a grave and up in heaven at the same time?

But Jake's yelling as he ran up the lane, waving something white in his hand, stopped her from thinking further. Slowly she splashed through the muddy yard toward him. Maybe Peter Klassen had brought some mail from town.

"Look!" Jake waved the piece of paper. "A letter from Aunt Carrie. Guess what, Martha? She's leaving Russia and will come to Kansas!"

"Will she live with us?" Martha asked eagerly, remembering papa's youngest sister, who was about twenty years old. Aunt Carrie had curly dark hair, laughing eyes, and dimpled cheeks.

Jake was still reading. "That's what she says. I think you can stop crying now, Martha. When Aunt Carrie comes, you won't be lonely anymore."

GRAY FOX

AFTER BREAKFAST THE FOLLOWING MONDAY, papa suggested that he and Martha pick elderberries so mama could make jelly for the coming winter. Jake had left a few days before, and mama was well enough to sit in the walnut rocker and sew. She still looked pale, but she smiled and even hummed a little as she stitched.

"I will fix the dinner when I come back, mama," Martha said as she reached for the gray enameled pail on the shelf above the stove.

Mama looked up. "*Eeee,* Martha, I can fix it myself—a big kettleful of bean soup."

Soup again! Martha frowned. She was tired of soup, but she knew there were still plenty of vegetables in the garden.

Carrying the pail, she followed papa out of the lean-to and over the yard to the pasture. He lifted the strands of barbed wire so she could crawl under, warning her to be careful not to tear her old gray chambray dress.

She almost had to run to keep up with papa's long strides. Beyond the hill across the pasture, Cottonwood Creek meandered through the fields for miles, even through the area where they used to live. At places, the stream was wide, and Jake said there was good trapping, especially during winter months.

Soon they reached the pleasant creek. Sunlight filtered through the leaves, falling on the quiet green water to make dark patterns. They could hear the noisy scolding of blue jays above the soft, swishy sounds of bass and catfish winnowing through the water. Papa walked ahead, parting the brush for Martha when it grew thick. She knew elderberries grew sweet and luscious just around the bend, and she stumbled and slid, trying to keep up.

Finally she tumbled to her knees. As she looked up, she saw an outstretched brown arm in the tall grass and heard a muffled groan.

"Papa!" she screamed. "Papa!"

He whirled around and looked at her with a puzzled frown. "What's wrong, Martha? Can't you keep up?"

"Look!" she pointed. "Somebody . . ." The words died in her throat.

Papa parted the grass brusquely and knelt down. "Gray Fox!" he murmured.

Martha crawled over beside papa. The Indian friend who had helped them time after time lay there unconscious, his faded red tunic streaked with dried mud and his black hair matted and tousled. A necklace of tiny shells hung around his neck.

Papa ran gentle fingers over the Indian's arms, then swiftly pointed to one twisted leg, clad in dun-colored trousers.

"His leg is broken, I'm sure," papa said.

"What can we do for him, papa? Can we carry him home?"

The Indian grunted, awakened by their voices. "Take Gray Fox . . . to house by riverside."

Martha stood up and looked about. She spied a dugout in the hillside not far away. Gray Fox probably camped there while he fished and trapped.

"His dugout's there, papa!" she cried.

"Why don't you see if you can find a blanket? Then we'll fashion a stretcher with poles and move him."

She stumbled through the brush and made her way to Gray Fox's dugout. The door stood open, and she paused in the frame to look around. Its one room contained a crude table with a stump for a seat. An old gray horse blanket lay neatly folded in one corner. Quickly she grabbed the blanket and hurried back to papa, who was splinting Gray Fox's leg with thin willow thongs and strips of his own denim shirt. She helped him fix a hammock with the blanket and some dried branches, and together they lifted the Indian into it. Gray Fox clenched his fists in pain but did not scream out. Then they dragged him to his dugout, where papa made him as comfortable as possible in one corner.

"Martha," he said after the Indian seemed to be resting quietly. "I want you to go home and fetch some of mama's good bean soup and fresh bread."

She looked at Gray Fox's pain-filled eyes, and tears rose in her own. The Indian raised one hand slightly, and a feeble smile touched his tight lips.

"Do not cry, white girl. Gray Fox soon be well."

She turned around and sped across the fields toward the barnyard, remembering how Gray Fox had killed a rattlesnake that would have bitten her. Later he had saved her cousin Ben Goertz's life after a rattler bit him. She was glad to do something for him now.

Martha stumbled across the yard and into

the lean-to. Mama was stirring a batch of bread in a huge stone bowl on the kitchen table.

"Mama, it's Gray Fox!" Between gulps for air, she told her mother what had happened. Before she finished, mama had wiped her hands and taken out a loaf of bread from the stone crock.

"Run to the fraidy cave for some butter," she said, slicing the bread into thick wedges.

Martha ran behind the house to the cave, hurried down the cool stone steps, and fumbled in the darkness for the crock of butter. She brought it back into the house and helped mama spread the butter onto the bread slices. Then she picked up a tin pail of hot vegetable soup and set out across the fields again.

The sun had grown warm, and sweat beaded her forehead under her bonnet. She remembered how Alice's mother had offered a paper pattern and a scrap of pink gingham for a bonnet to keep the sun off her face. But she had worn the bonnet so much it was now almost white.

Finally she entered Gray Fox's dugout. He watched her pour soup into a tin plate and lay out the buttered slices of bread. Then he pointed to a tin pail. "Bubbling water down hill," he grunted.

Bubbling water? A spring, probably.

Martha hurried outside and found the spring easily. She rinsed out the pail and filled it with water that gurgled, fresh and clear, from beneath a rock.

For the next several days, she brought food to the Indian, who always seemed glad to see her. He did not talk much but listened as she told him of the day's happenings.

Once she spoke of Baby Franz. "We buried him in the little graveyard near the woods."

"Baby sleep under sod," Gray Fox murmured, nodding.

"Well—papa says he's not really under the sod, but up in heaven with Jesus. I don't quite understand."

"Do you have black book telling of Great Spirit?" he asked.

"Black book? Oh, a Bible. Yes, we have several, but they are in the German language."

When she told papa about this later, he remembered Jake had forgotten to take his English New Testament with him.

"Why don't you take it along next time and read to Gray Fox?"

"Do you think he would understand, papa?"

"The Indian is smart. He knows more than we might think." Papa patted her shoulder.

The next day she told him she had brought the black book. "Shall I read to you?" she asked.

He nodded and listened patiently as she read of Jesus' miracles. One day after she had read the story of Jesus dying on the cross, he turned to her.

"Why did white man put Jesus on cross?"

Martha sighed. How did one explain that, especially when neither of them spoke English well? "I guess it was because we do bad things sometimes. But God loved us so much he sent Jesus to die for us so we could be forgiven."

Gray Fox was silent for a long time. Then he said, "Gray Fox does bad things, too. How can Jesus change that?"

Martha did not know how to explain it. She remembered that Peter Wiebe had said someone should tell the Indians Jesus loved them so they could believe, too.

When she returned home, she asked her father if Indians could become Christians. "Peter Wiebe once said so," she continued, "but he said the Sioux and Osage could not understand Low German, so they would probably never hear of God's love."

Papa looked at her. "I cannot speak English very good, Martha, so if Gray Fox wants to learn more, you will have to teach him!"

Ach, if only I can help him, she thought.

10
PEOPLE OF
THE SOUTH WIND

MARTHA CROSSED THE FIELDS to Gray Fox's dugout every day with soups or other foods from mama's kitchen. Often she read several chapters from Jake's New Testament. Sometimes he asked questions; other times he simply nodded, his dark eyes intense.

There were times when he entertained her by imitating the sounds of birds and animals that lived on the prairies: the chirp of a sparrow, the hoot of an owl, the warble of the meadowlark, and the howl of a coyote. When Gray Fox croaked like a frog, she always felt it was going to rain, because Jake had told her that frogs' croaking was a sure sign of rain.

Once Gray Fox began to hobble around again, Martha knew he would soon be on his own. She would miss their visits, because he had become a trusted friend.

Summer had sped by quickly, and now it was late August. For weeks papa had been plowing the wheat stubble, walking behind the single plow to guide the plowshare as it turned over a furrow at a time of the rich black loam. Many times Martha had filled the burlap-covered jug with water from the well and hurried across the field to bring him a cold drink. Crossing the gypsy stream that wandered through the pale yellow squares of stubble, she had breathed deeply of air that was now heavy with the smell of damp earth, wheat straw, and the aroma of purple alfalfa.

If Aunt Carrie had not come soon after Gray Fox left, Martha might have become lonely again. But now her aunt's arrival was only a few days away. Martha had scrubbed the wood floor of her tiny bedroom and cleaned her closet.

Then on the day her aunt was to arrive, she announced to mama, "I want Aunt Carrie to stay in my room." She puffed up her feather bed and then continued. "I hope she stays forever."

Mama gave a final swipe to the already shining north window. "*Eeee,* don't make her promise anything foolish, Martha."

"Foolish! But this time I want to keep my friend," she said firmly. "First I lost Alice, then Baby Franz. I don't want to be disappointed again."

Without a word, mama picked up her scrub bucket and left the room. Martha finished making the bed and followed her into the dining room. Every corner of the house was spotless, even the crowded lean-to.

Papa had already left for the railroad station to meet Aunt Carrie's train. Martha set the dining room table with the best dishes; this was a very special occasion. They ate in the lean-to when they were alone, but now that papa had been elected an elder in the church, they would invite company often.

Just as she tied a fresh apron around her waist, she heard the wagon creak up the lane. Quickly she raced out the lean-to door and through the gate. The minute papa stopped the team, Aunt Carrie jumped from the wagon, and they were hugging each other.

Martha sniffed her aunt's soft blue dress and turned up her nose. "You smell of cinders and soot and stale tobacco. Is that how trains smell?"

Aunt Carrie threw her head back and laughed. "Why, Martha, you haven't changed a bit. Always the prissy little miss!"

Aunt Carrie chattered in Low German. She looked just as Martha remembered her: the brown hair that curled softly in a fringe around her dimpled cheeks, the merry blue eyes, and the saucy, laughing mouth. Even though she was almost twenty years old, Aunt Carrie bubbled with fun.

Now she held Martha away from her. "*Na,* Martha, I thought I would see a wild prairie flower, growing out of a chink in the sod house. What do I find? The same red rose that left Russia, complete with a few thorns!" She laughed again. "You ought to get that light back into your eyes and laugh a little now and then."

"But Baby Franz—"

"Uh-uh. Aunt Carrie's here, and there's no room for tears. Your papa tells me you have been helping an—Indian. Didn't he scare you to death?"

"Gray Fox?" Martha paused to open the gate. "Why should I be afraid of him? He's our friend."

Aunt Carrie walked ahead of Martha. The delicious smell of chicken frying drifted out to meet them. At least it wasn't soup this time, Martha thought, and almost laughed at herself. Having Aunt Carrie here would make a lot of things feel right, no matter what there was to eat.

After dinner, mama lay down for a nap, and Martha turned to her aunt. "You must be tired. Would you like to nap, too?"

Aunt Carrie laughed. "Who, me? Not a bit. I'd rather have you show me around. I can't wait to see it all. There's so much space. But this wind! How can you stand it?"

Martha threw out her hands. "The wind is what gives Kansas its name. It was named for the *Kanza* Indians—'people of the south wind.' But it's not windy every day."

Martha led her aunt out to see the barn. The smell of leather and oats was strong in the stalls. As curious as ever, Aunt Carrie scooped up her long full skirt and clambered into the hayloft. Martha followed her.

"Say, this must be a nice place to come when you want to be alone," Aunt Carrie said as she plopped down on the fragrant piles of hay.

"No," Martha said, shaking her head. "I go to the woods. It's dark and cool there, and I can be by myself. Sometimes I go to Baby Franz's grave.

"Well, I'd rather see the woods." She scrambled to her feet and started down the ladder. Martha led the way through the windy yard and down the narrow path behind the hen house. Once they got to the woods, Martha hurried to the old log and brushed off the driblets of dirt.

"Let's sit here and talk."

Aunt Carrie spread out her skirts, curtsied, and then seated herself with a great deal of aplomb. "The Grand Empress of Moscow is holding court!" she cried.

Martha stood beside her, growing happier by the minute. She hoped her aunt would never leave.

Just then she heard the familiar clop-clop of Abram Petker's horse, and she spun around with a frown on her face.

"*Ach,* not him!" she muttered. "I hope—"

"*Hui,* and what are you doing in the woods, Martha Friesen?" he shouted, jumping from his horse. "You haven't been out to your brother's grave today, have you?" He paused, catching sight of Aunt Carrie seated on the log, her skirts spread out in a half-circle.

Martha looked from Aunt Carrie to the young man in front of her. She knew she must introduce them. "This is my Aunt Carrie. She just arrived from the Ukraine." Martha faltered. She hoped Abram would go away. Instead, he gave a low whistle and bowed.

"Well, how pleasant," he said, his dark eyes flashing. He began to chatter endlessly about the prairie, his wheat, his horse, and his dogs. He never ran out of words.

Aunt Carrie lowered her eyes, then cut in sharply. "You are right, Martha. I see how winds do give Kansas its name!"

Abram's face grew red, and he whirled around angrily and left.

"What was that all about, Aunt Carrie?"

For a long time the young woman was silent. Then she smiled. "Well, there are windbags, you know—people who only want to talk about themselves." She jumped up suddenly. "I want you to show me your baby brother's grave. Then you can help me unpack. I hope I can stay here for a long time, Martha—wind or no wind!" She laughed again.

So do I, Martha thought. She had almost forgotten the tiny grave in the cemetery.

11
THAT ODD
YOUNG MAN

Aunt Carrie and Martha—what fun they had together. They picked beans and hoed the garden. Aunt Carrie taught her how to piece quilt tops from scraps of dark blue percale and unbleached feed sacks.

Sometimes they sang funny folk songs like *"Rooszhe-batrooszhe, waut rushchelt em Stroh?"* ("Say, goodness me, what's rustling in the straw?") Aunt Carrie's voice quavered sadly as she sang about the poor little goslings who had no shoes. And Martha laughed until tears filled her eyes.

One day they built a playhouse under the mulberry trees near the hen house. They used markings in the soft dirt for rooms and bits of broken china as dishes.

"Na, what's this queer thing, Martha?" Aunt Carrie asked, holding a white triangle

she had found on the ground. "I've never seen anything like this before."

Martha scratched her head. She could not think of a single Low German word to describe an Indian arrowhead. Taking it in her hand, she turned it over thoughtfully. Finally she said, "The Indians used to carve these things from flint rock. They fixed them onto sticks and then used bows to shoot them at buffalo . . . or people."

"People!" Aunt Carrie shrieked. "I hope they've gotten over that habit by now."

"Of course. I've told you about Gray Fox."

"You said you visited him every day. I'd be scared to pieces. Has he recovered from his broken leg?"

Martha laughed. "*Ach,* yes, he's fine now. I told you he's a good friend. And when he likes you, he lets you know."

"But he's a heathen, isn't he? How can you be friends—"

"Oh, he'll probably never come to the Mennonite church, because he can't understand German. But I read to him from Jake's English New Testament. God loves him anyhow, papa says."

"I guess he does," Aunt Carrie said slowly. Then she looked at the sky. "The sun is slanting toward the west, and I'd better get into the house and help your mother fix supper. You

77

can stay and play awhile." She started for the house.

Martha watched her go. She decided to visit Baby Franz's grave. It had been a long time since she had been there. She crawled through the fence and padded to the little mound. Already bindweed and crabgrass had begun to creep through the cracks, and she yanked them out.

"Out . . . you . . . go," she muttered aloud. "And don't you dare grow back!"

"And why not? They're just weeds," a mocking voice said from behind her. She jerked around and there stood Abram Petker, his dark eyes blazing.

Martha pressed her lips together firmly. Didn't Abram have anything to do but snoop around on their land?

He laughed. "Don't look so high-hat. By the way, where's your fine-looking aunt?"

"She's helping mama cook supper," Martha said with a frown.

"Well, now, she wouldn't be interested in talking to a fine, upstanding young man, would she?"

"Where? I don't see any."

His face darkened. "You know whom I mean, Martha Friesen. Some day I'm going to marry her. I want you to ask her if she will let me visit her."

"But Aunt Carrie's not going to leave us—ever!" Martha cried. "She came to keep me company."

"*Hui,* did she?" he laughed harshly. "When a pretty girl reaches her age, she doesn't live with her family forever. Not when there are nice young men around. You ought to know that."

"But she promised! She said—"

"There's plenty of land to be had right in this area," he cut in. "Not all the homesteads are taken. If we got married, we could live on the next farm, and you could see her every day. Wouldn't you like that?"

Martha traced lines in the dirt with her finger. "That's not for me to say."

"But will you ask her?"

She wiggled her feet and stared for a long time at the horizon. The sun had dipped toward the west, painting the sky in red and orange. The shreds of clouds looked as though they had caught fire. She turned to Abram and nodded slightly.

"*Ja,* I will mention it to her. But that's all."

Picking up her full skirt, she ran to the fence, scrambled through, and raced across the yard. She hoped she had not torn her gray chambray in her hurry to get away from Abram.

She raced into the lean-to, where Aunt Carrie stirred fried potatoes in a heavy skillet over the fire.

"You won't, will you?" Martha cried, her eyes troubled and anxious.

"I won't what, Martha?" Aunt Carrie looked up from the stove, her merry face flushed from the heat.

"Move away from here. Abram Petker seems to think—well, he told me to ask you . . ." she faltered.

Aunt Carrie laid her spoon down and placed her hands on Martha's shoulders. "Now, just what is it your neighbor has in mind?" She laughed, and then she picked up her spoon again. "You ought to stay away from that odd young man, Martha," she warned.

"Then you won't leave?" Martha asked, not listening to her aunt's warning.

"Not for a long, long time. Now, why don't you help by setting the supper table? You can set that bread crock in the corner."

Martha was relieved. As she cleared the table and began to set out the dishes, she smiled a little. Aunt Carrie was right, and she would not worry about it again.

When papa came in, he was full of news. "Sunday we're having a special day in church. A preacher from Nebraska is visiting, and we will have an all-day service. He will preach twice, and the whole congregation will eat dinner together—ham and cherry moos and butter bread."

Martha was busy for the next two days, helping her aunt and mother with preparations for Sunday. She did not even get out to the woods. Since Abram Petker almost never came to church, she probably would not have to give him Carrie's answer.

But when the family drove up to the church on Sunday, Abram was already there, his dark hair slicked back and his white shirt starched and stiff. He smirked all during the preaching as though everything was already arranged between him and Aunt Carrie.

At noon Aunt Carrie helped set the meal out on desks that had been pushed together.

"Your aunt looks very pretty," Liesbet Wiens told Martha as they herded the little tots out to the shady side of the building. "She will find a man, and before you know it, there will be a wedding here in this schoolhouse!"

Martha frowned. Couldn't anyone understand? Aunt Carrie had not come to America to find a husband.

"*Ja,* she is very pretty, and I'm proud of her," Martha said finally. "She's such a happy person to have around."

"And a big help, too," Liesbet added. "See how she's helping the ladies?"

Aunt Carrie was hauling water up from the

cistern with a rope. Martha saw Abram Petker hurry toward her, and Martha's mouth grew dry. *I have to stall him off,* she thought.

"Abram, Abram!" she yelled, pointing to a rock. "I thought I saw a rattler over there!"

Abram turned and rushed toward her. "Where?"

Martha held her breath. She had not seen a snake, but she had to get Abram away from Aunt Carrie. She glanced toward the cistern. Aunt Carrie was already hurrying back into the schoolhouse.

"I—" She bit her lower lip. "I guess I was mistaken. There was no snake after all."

He whirled on her angrily. "You!" he hissed, grabbing her roughly. "You just wanted to keep me away from your aunt, didn't you?" He shook her hard.

Martha jerked away and thrust her chin out sharply. "Well, she won't marry you anyway. She said so!"

"Oh, did she now?" He placed his hands on his hips, his black eyes wild. "We'll see. Give me time. Something terrible is going to happen if she doesn't. And don't you forget that!"

He swung around and stalked away angrily. Martha's eyes followed him, and she shivered. What terrible thing could happen?

"Something terrible is going to happen."

12
A SECRET TRIP

FOR FOUR DAYS papa and mama had spoken
in hushed tones when they thought they were
alone. But when Martha came into the room,
they grew quiet. Often mama placed her hand
on Martha's forehead and looked at her
strangely.

"What is going on, Aunt Carrie?" Martha
asked one day while they hoed weeds that had
cropped up between the corn rows. "Why is
mama always feeling my forehead?"

Aunt Carrie leaned against her hoe. "*Ach,*
Martha, I suppose you don't know, but there's
a bad sickness going around called
diphtheria. People, especially children, suddenly become very ill with fever and sore
throat. Some choke to death because of the

swelling. Some have already died. . . . I guess you heard about Susie Epp."

Martha nodded. She remembered gawky twelve-year-old Susie, who lived several miles from their old farm. Now Susie's gabby tongue was forever still.

Aunt Carrie went on. "The sickness is very catching, and in some families all the children have caught it. Which means we go nowhere except to church."

"But won't it be catching in church?"

Aunt Carrie shrugged. "Surely God won't permit that!"

Martha fell silent. She hoped none of the Friesens would get this dread sickness. Only the *scritch-scritch* of her hoe broke the stillness of the afternoon.

"Is that why Annie Isaac wasn't in church yesterday?" she asked suddenly. "Is she sick?"

"Uh—" Aunt Carrie kept her eye on a stubborn cockleburr that resisted the hoe. "Not Annie, but her little sister Marie. None of the medicines Dr. Enns has given has helped. It looks grim."

Martha's hoe *scritched* on. The sun shone hot, and sweat dampened the back of her neck. She took off her bonnet and waved it back and forth to dry her wet face. She knew how much Annie would miss little Marie if she died. Just as she missed Baby Franz—and she had not even known him, except in her dreams.

After the last corn row was done, the girls walked home. Martha was tired. As she hurried into the lean-to, she tossed her sunbonnet on the table and headed for the water bucket. She dipped out water, fresh from the well, and sipped it slowly, letting it trickle down her throat. As she drank, she overheard someone talking in the dining room. No one but Gerta Harms's bulky mother spoke with such a breathy voice.

"*Ja,*" the woman said heavily, "the little Tinsley girl is very sick. Doctor says it will be a miracle if she lives. The dread diphtheria takes Mennonite and non-Mennonite alike. Only our Lord knows why."

Martha froze. Alice Tinsley—diphtheria? Even though she and Alice had not seen each other all summer, they would always be best friends. Alice could not die. She mustn't! Martha rushed outside to be alone.

Papa strolled over to the picket gate, taking two milk pails that hung overturned on the gate posts. He eyed her sharply.

"*Na,* Martha, why the tears? Was hoeing corn so hard?" he asked kindly.

She shook her head as she cleared her throat to speak. "*Ach,* papa, I heard mama and Mrs. Harms talking about Alice Tinsley. She has diphtheria, papa. I must go to her."

"No, Martha!" Papa's voice was firm. "You cannot see her. She is far too sick. If you would catch her sickness—"

"But Alice is my best friend! I have to see her."

Papa set his milk pails on the ground and placed his leathery hands on her cheeks. "Martha, we cannot allow it. Please believe me. We know what's best."

"But papa—"

"No!" he thundered. Turning away, he picked up his pails and strode swiftly toward the barn. Martha's eyes followed him, tears blurring her vision. If only there were a way . . .

Stumbling across the yard toward the woods, she was scarcely aware of the thistles that clawed at her bare feet. She had to get away, to cry where nobody heard her. Finding her favorite log, she sat down and covered her face with her arms.

"Well, now what's wrong?" A familiar voice sounded behind her. Why was Abram Petker always out here when she wanted to be alone? At first she did not reply, but she could not keep the news to herself.

"*Ach,* it's my best friend, Alice Tinsley. She has diphtheria. I must go to her. But papa says he cannot allow it!"

"Why do you have to see her, Martha?"

"Because she may die. What if I never see her again?"

He nodded. "I see. Tell you what. Come here tomorrow morning, and I'll take you to Tinsleys' on my horse. But you must promise to tell no one. They wouldn't let you go, you know."

"I'm sure they wouldn't. But if you'd do that, Abram, you're nicer than I thought."

He grinned wryly. "I figured you'd catch on. Some day you will tell your pretty aunt how great I really am!" Then he swung around and left.

Martha hurried back to the house, feeling much better now that she would see Alice in the morning. But part of her remembered her aunt's warning about Abram Petker. She was disobeying papa and her aunt.

That night she tossed restlessly in bed. Her dreams were clogged with golden-haired girls who choked and gasped and coughed. Finally it was morning.

After papa had gone to the barn and mama and Aunt Carrie had lugged tubs of hot, soapy water out back, Martha slipped into the woods. Minutes later, Abram rode up on his horse. He helped her up, warning her to hang on.

They rode slowly past the little cemetery and around to the south road. Then they turned west. The sun beat hot on Martha's back, and soon sweat soaked her dress.

Meadowlarks darted from the fence rows, and great masses of yellow and purple, daisylike Indian Blanket carpeted the road sides, making a bright splash of color along the shallow ditches.

After some time Martha could see the roof of Tinsleys' store. How dear the familiar place looked! She hoped it was not too late to see Alice.

"I'll come back in half an hour," Abram told her. "We need some things from the store." He reined in sharply before the square white house, and Martha slid from the horse's back. Then she rushed to the kitchen door and rapped impatiently. After what felt like some time, Mrs. Tinsley came to the door. She looked gaunt and tired.

"Martha!" she cried. "What are you doing here?"

"I came to see Alice. I heard she was very sick."

"Oh, no, you can't come in. She's much too ill. Diphtheria spreads so fast; we dare not allow it!"

"But I must see her!" Martha wailed. "Just for a few minutes. Please?"

Mrs. Tinsley turned away quickly and slammed the door. Martha checked to see that

Abram's horse was still tethered outside the store. Then she went behind the house to sit in the rope swing. Would no one believe how much Alice meant to her?

Just then Mrs. Tinsley came out of the house and hurried along the cinder path that led to the store. As she disappeared through the doorway, Martha tiptoed to the kitchen and let herself in. The shadowy room, now acrid with the smell of camomile tea and sulphur, made her blink. Then she moved quietly into Alice's tiny bedroom, remembering the fun they had shared here.

Alice lay white and still, her eyes closed. The faint rise and fall of her chest told Martha she was alive. Bending over her friend, Martha whispered, "Alice . . . Alice, it's Martha. Can you see me?"

Alice gave no sign she knew Martha was there. Sometimes her throat rattled as she breathed, and Martha shuddered, remembering Aunt Carrie's words about people choking to death. Martha tore her sunbonnet off and knelt beside the bed. Why didn't God make Alice well?

Then Martha felt the bed stir. Color seeped into Alice's white cheeks as her eyelids fluttered, and she opened her eyes.

"Mar—tha . . . I'm so glad . . . you're here," she mumbled. "Please—don't go away. Please stay here with me. . . ."

"Oh, Alice!" Martha cried. "I'll stay as long as I can! I'm so glad you woke up. I was afraid—"

"Martha, I'm going—to get well. I saw Jesus . . . and many other people, big and small. They looked so happy I wanted to stay, but he sent me back."

Martha gulped. People! If she saw people in heaven, surely . . . "Did you see my baby brother, Alice? Was Franz there?" she asked eagerly.

Alice shook her head slightly. "I don't remember. No, I don't think I saw him. But . . ." Her voice faded.

Martha was shaken. Did that mean Baby Franz was still in the grave? Martha rose slowly to her feet, the question drifting through her mind as she and Abram rode toward home.

13

DIPHTHERIA!

W HEN SHE RETURNED to the house, mama met her at the gate.

"Martha, where have you been? We called and called, and you didn't come." Her voice was stern.

Martha bit her lip sharply. She should have known she would be missed. "Did you want me for something?"

"I needed you to hang the clothes out," mama said in an anxious voice. "If you went to visit Gray Fox, you should have told us."

Martha shook her head. She took her sunbonnet off and swung it by the strings as she started toward the lean-to.

"I didn't go to see Gray Fox, mama. I went—" She paused a moment and then plunged on. "I went to see Alice."

"You *what*?" Mama whispered hoarsely. "You went to see Alice Tinsley when you knew she had diphtheria? . . . Why?"

"I love Alice, mama. I had to see her, especially since she might die. Abram Petker offered to take me on his horse. . . ." Martha shook so now that she could not continue. The frightened look on mama's face scared her. Just outside the lean-to mama laid a firm hand on her shoulder.

"That Abram Petker needs a whipping. Don't you know—" mama's voice broke, then she continued in the same shrill tone. "You can get this terrible illness from her. More and more people are dying every day."

"But Alice isn't going to die, mama," Martha said. "She was so happy I came."

"Didn't you think of yourself—of us—when you went there?"

Martha shook her head stubbornly. "I just wanted to see her, mama."

"Even after papa forbade you! The sickness comes in three or four days. May God grant that you be spared!" Mama jerked her hand away and walked slowly back to her washboard behind the house.

Martha avoided meeting papa's eyes when he came in for dinner. She sat with her head bowed and pushed her food around on her plate. She had always liked corn, fresh from the field and dribbling with butter; today the ears tasted flat and dull.

After the meal papa got up from the table and stood beside her. His eyes looked angry, but he controlled his voice. "Martha, you know you disobeyed me, even after I told you not to see Alice. I know your love for her overshadowed your concern for your own health and my orders."

"Yes, papa."

"But when I think—" His voice thickened, but he choked his emotion back. "When I think that in a few days you may come down with the dread diphtheria like so many others . . ." His voice broke.

Suddenly Martha slipped out of her chair and grabbed the homemade fly swatter from its nail on the wall.

"Here, papa. I know I deserve to be punished. Spank me hard. Please, papa?"

Papa looked at her, his eyes full of love and his bearded chin quivering. Then he threw his arms around her and hugged her tight.

"*Na,* Martha. We will trust God in whatever comes. Our only hope is in him." Then he went out of the house toward the barn.

After dinner papa and Aunt Carrie drove to town, taking cream and eggs to trade for sugar and flour. Martha finished the dishes and hung the dishpan up. Then she jammed the sunbonnet over her wheat-colored hair and went outside. Fromm, who was drowsing in the shade, got up to nuzzle his nose against her skirt. Suddenly he began to bark, and Martha looked toward the road. Eli Petker shuffled up the lane, his bare feet dragging in the dust and his hair tousling in the wind.

"Hello, Martha," he called when he reached their gate. He thrust out a chipped enamel pan. "Ma wants to borrow a few eggs if you can spare them."

"Papa took the eggs to town, but there are usually a few hens in the hayloft. Maybe I can find some for you."

Eli wiggled his toes in the dirt. "Abram tells me you went to see Alice Tinsley this morning. Did you get a lickin' because you disobeyed your pa?"

"Papa forgave me when he realized I thought only about Alice. I didn't know my folks would be so upset."

"Diphtheria is a bad sickness," Eli went on. "I guess you heard about Mrs. Klassen?"

"No."

"She died this morning. Pa heard it when he drove over to use their corn sheller."

Martha's neck grew hot. She recalled the night she had spent at the Klassens' when Baby Franz was born. Mrs. Klassen had been so kind; now she was gone.

Will I be next? she thought. Slowly she took the pan from Eli and went to the barn, where she found three eggs, warm and brown, in the fragrant hay.

She was very quiet the next few days. Every time she felt tired or a little hot, she was afraid she might be getting diphtheria. But as the days dragged by and the dreaded symptoms did not appear, she stopped worrying. Before long she forgot about the illness, except to make sure that Alice had improved.

One day Aunt Carrie told the family, "I'm going to work for Peter Klassen. His youngsters need someone to look after them, and there is no one else. He has promised to pay my wages in calves."

Martha was stunned. "Do you mean you will leave us? But I thought—"

"I'm not leaving, Martha!" Her dark eyes sparkled, and she laughed. "I will come back every night. I need to earn some money, since I have nothing of my own. After I sell the calves, I will buy some clothes. This wind blows my aprons to shreds! And look at my shoes. I'm as bad as the barefoot goslings!"

"But I won't see you—" Martha began.

"Be thankful you are well, Martha. I will be here on Sundays; Mr. Klassen will not need me then."

Martha nodded. She knew her aunt was right. She had not gotten sick, and Alice was getting better. She had a lot to be thankful for.

14
ROBIN HOOD

MARTHA PICKED UP a syrup pail with butter bread sandwiches inside and hurried out the door. Today was her first day of school in the Warren Schoolhouse. Eli and Sam Petker were already ambling down the road, their homemade trousers hoisted up with pieces of twine, their unruly hair slicked back.

"Hoo!" she shouted. "Wait for me!" She ran down the dusty road to catch up. How different the walk to school was going to be. At their other house so many little farms had been scattered along the road, it was almost like a village. But now only the Nickel children joined them—tall Ben, plump little Sarah, and their leggy twin sisters.

"What reader are you in?" Sarah asked as she walked beside Martha. "Or can't you read yet?"

"Read?" Martha laughed. "Not as good in English as in German, but I think I'll be in the fourth reader."

"The fourth! Then you can help me. Do you know the teacher?"

Martha paused to watch a beetle that scurried across the road. "Miss Gibbs? No, but I hear she doesn't know any German. Have you met her?"

"Not yet, but she's probably a big bossy lady. She'd have to be to handle the older boys!"

"Most likely she'll stick up for the English pupils who aren't Mennonites," Ben grouched, swinging his dinner pail in an arc. Martha knew he was wishing for a Mennonite school, like they had attended in Russia and their first year here.

"I wonder how many pupils will be there?" Eli muttered as he started after a yellow butterfly that finally darted into a clump of goldenrod.

"It depends," Ben replied. "At least fifty or sixty. After the corn is in, some of the other big boys will come. I hope I'm not the only one who's seventeen."

Several others joined them, and by the time they reached the schoolyard, children were coming from every direction. Martha had met many of them in church.

When the bell rang, Martha left her syrup
pail on the shelf in the hall and entered the
schoolroom. A tiny woman with frizzy brown
hair sat behind the teacher's desk in the front.
She's not what Sarah expected, Martha
thought.

School began with several songs and the
Lord's Prayer. As the morning wore on, the
schoolhouse grew stuffy. A breeze blew in
through the open windows, carrying the smell
of the endless prairie as it fluttered the pages
of the readers on the desks.

Martha fidgeted. The other fifty-four pupils
seemed restless, too. Ben Nickel snickered out
loud, although he behaved. Ed Bates, another
older boy, grew noisy. And big Herman Engle
tripped Annie Isaac so she fell in the aisle,
cutting her lip on the sharp corner of her desk.
During recess Herman erased the teacher's
arithmetic problems from the blackboard and
dumped a bucket of drinking water on the
floor.

"That's enough, Herman," Miss Gibbs said
firmly. "Maybe you'd like to get another pail
of water for us."

Herman refused to move, encouraged by
Ben's snickering and Ed Bates, who shoved
Eli into Herman's seat.

The days that followed were worse. Herman
knocked over Liesbet Wiens's inkwell and

splashed ink all over her new gray chambray. He jiggled elbows as he tried to copy others' slatework, and he refused to obey Miss Gibbs.

Finally Martha, Annie, and Liesbet approached Miss Gibbs one morning when the others were out at recess.

"Teacher," Martha said shyly, trying to use her best English. "We were wondering . . . well, Herman Engle is upsetting everything. Can't you tell him to go home and never come back?"

"No," Miss Gibbs said, shaking her head firmly.

"But why not?" Annie burst out. "He made me fall and cut my lip, and he spilled ink on Liesbet's dress. He's done lots of awful things."

Miss Gibbs smiled dully. "Herman has as much right to be here as the rest of you."

"Then what are you going to do?" Annie asked.

"I'll think of something," the teacher replied in a soft voice. "You girls had better go out and play. Recess is nearly over."

The next day the sixth grade began reading *Robin Hood*. They read how Robin and Little John met on a bridge and fought with staffs to see who would fall in the water first. As they read, Miss Gibbs drew a paddle from her desk drawer.

"This is how they must have sparred," she chattered, waving it back and forth. She inched her way toward Herman. Before anyone realized what was happening, she began to hit his hands and his shoulders, not with full force, of course, but enough to make Herman think. And all the while Miss Gibbs went on describing Robin Hood's fight! Herman's plump face became dark red, but he did not move to stop her.

At recess he stood outside and blubbered, "Didn't think she'd have the nerve. I thought she was afraid to touch me."

When Martha walked home with the Petkers and the Nickels that night, even Ben admitted, "Maybe she's English, but she sure knows how to manage our school!"

"You were lucky she didn't punish you for snickering," Martha added tartly. "Maybe next time—"

"Next time won't come," Ben grumbled. "Guess I'll learn all I can this year, so pa will let me take next year off. By then I'll know everything, anyway."

15

STRANGE MEDICINE

OCTOBER MOVED SILENTLY BY, with the heavy scent of drying hay and ripening apples and the smell of freshly plowed earth. One day Martha dragged in from school and flung her bonnet in one corner.

"*Na*, Martha," mama said as she peeled tart yellow apples at the kitchen table. "The floor is not the place for bonnets."

"*Ach*, mama, I know," Martha muttered wearily. Her head ached and she felt very tired. As she stooped to pick her bonnet up, she grew dizzy and had to steady herself.

Mama looked at her curiously. "Are you sick, Martha?"

Without answering, she stumbled into her bedroom and threw herself on the bed. She wanted to sleep and could not wake up to eat any of the tasty soup mama brought, or the milk she coaxed Martha to sip.

Through the dimness of the next few days,

she felt mama place cool, wet cloths on her forehead. But they made her feel no better. Then one day a strange face blurred in front of her as his hands thumped and tested. She heard a far-off voice say, "It's the crippling sickness."

"Dear God . . ." mama's voice prayed in an agonizing tone. "Are you sure, Dr. Enns?"

"Yes, I am sure. She may come out of it with no crippling at all, or she could become completely helpless. We cannot tell," the doctor admitted. "Her left arm and leg are somewhat paralyzed. Keep the others out of this room until the fever is gone," he warned, and then he left.

As the days wore on, Martha's head stopped hurting, and she grew hungry for mama's soups again. But Dr. Enns was right: she could barely move her left arm and leg.

Each evening when Aunt Carrie came home from work, she sat by Martha's bed and told her stories or sang funny songs. She made a game of trying to get Martha to raise her left arm—like playing Dutch windmill and waving her arms. But the left arm refused to move.

"Let's pretend you're a mule, Martha," she would say, "and you're supposed to plow. Now kick your feet!" Yet only the right foot would shoot into the air.

At first she liked being waited on. When she wanted a drink of water or a handful of dried apples, someone always hurried to her side. Her bed had been moved into the dining room so she was nearer to the family.

But as the weeks dragged on and she could not move her limbs, she began to worry.

"Will I ever walk again, mama?" she asked anxiously one day. "Or will I always lie in bed this way?"

A tear glimmered in mama's eyes. "Martha, it's up to God to answer that."

As Martha lay there, trying to pass another long day by memorizing Bible verses, she prayed. *I love these prairies, Jesus. Won't you let me walk through the tall grass again?*

Through the window Martha watched the yellow cottonwood leaves swirl to the ground. She saw Fromm chase them as gusts of wind blew across the yard. How she would love to run with him.

Then one day a frantic pounding sounded on the lean-to door. Mama hurried across the room to open it, and Martha saw a familiar bronze face framed by black hair that was held by a thong—Gray Fox. He came swiftly to her bed. "White girl sick?"

Martha touched her arm and leg. "I—can't move them, Gray Fox. . . ."

He stared at her for a long time, his steely

black eyes searching her face. Then he whirled around to face mama.

"Fix much hot water. I come back." Snatching an empty feed sack from a nail on the wall, he moved swiftly out of the room.

"*Eeee,* what does he want?" mama asked. She did not understand English, so Martha explained in Low German.

"He wants you to fix lots of hot water. I think he plans to help."

Martha watched as mama carried in bucketfuls of water from the well and poured them into the big iron kettle on the stove.

An hour later Gray Fox was back, carrying the sack. He got the wooden washtub and poured the hot water into it. Then he untied the partially filled sack and dumped some crumbled leaves into the water. He picked Martha up gently and carried her to the tub. Pulling up a backless chair, he sat down and inched her leg carefully into the hot water.

At first she cried, for the water was very hot. But knowing he wanted to help, she clenched her teeth and stifled her groans.

After a while, he lifted her out and motioned for the coarse towel that hung on a nail by the wash basin. He rubbed Martha's arm and leg with strong, vigorous strokes until they tingled. Then he carried her back to bed.

When he turned toward the door, he shook his long black hair out of his eyes. "I come back tomorrow and give more hot bath. But—" he eyed her sharply, "tell no one that Gray Fox come here!" Then he left as noiselessly as he had come. Martha begged to tell Aunt Carrie, but mama said no. They must respect Gray Fox's wishes.

For several weeks the Indian shuffled into the kitchen each morning with his sack of medicinal leaves and eased Martha into the hot water, toweling her left arm and leg briskly afterward.

Mama began to fix fresh butter bread for him each day, which he always ate with pleasure. Sometimes Martha heard the familiar warble of the meadowlark when he left. Other days he asked her to read from the black book.

Before long she could wiggle her toes and bend her fingers a little. Then one day, she tried to stand. At first the ground seemed far below her. But once her legs touched the floor, she was able to ease her weight onto them, slowly releasing her hold on mama and Gray Fox. Her legs quivered under the strain. But for the first time in over a month, she stood. Her left leg seemed thin and shriveled; but as the days went by, it grew stronger.

One day after Gray Fox had finished her treatment, he and Martha sat at the table

Gray Fox carried Martha gently to the tub.

eating butter bread. Suddenly a bullfrog's
kreak-kreak echoed through the lean-to, followed by the sound of running footsteps. Aunt
Carrie burst into the kitchen.

"Martha, do you know there's a frog in the
house?" Then she screamed. "What in the
world—" she stopped, her face white with hor-
ror.

Martha raised her left arm. "*Ach,* Aunt
Carrie, don't be scared. It's just Gray Fox."

Aunt Carrie came and stood beside the table, her mouth open. Then she stretched her
hand out in welcome.

Gray Fox unloosed his shell necklace and
laid it gently into her hand. "For you," he said
simply. Then he was on his feet and gone.

Aunt Carrie stared after him, at the shell
necklace in her hand, and at the tub of water.

"That Indian . . . that's how you've come to
walk?" she gasped.

Martha nodded, tears in her eyes. "When he
broke his leg, I took him food. Now he has
helped me. But he told me not to tell anyone."

"Still he wasn't angry when I came in,"
Aunt Carrie said. "And he gave me this—"
She held up the necklace.

"Because you stretched your hand out in
welcome," Martha explained, smiling.

16
BLACK SATEEN

CHRISTMAS WITH ITS SIMPLE HOMEMADE GIFTS and happy singing, came and went. Gray Fox had stopped his daily visits, but he told Martha to rub her arm and fingers every day, bending and flexing, and to work with her leg until the stiffness waned. By the time she was well enough to return to school, only a slight limp remained.

Snow fell the night before, settling on the barn and sheds and penciling the bare cottonwoods with thin white lines. In the morning, papa drove her to school, with a heavy robe tucked over her lap. The ruts along the road had been smoothed over by the snow's hard surface.

When Martha hobbled over the threshold, Miss Gibbs got up from her desk and hurried toward her. "It's good to have you back, Martha," she said smiling. "I hope you haven't fallen too far behind."

"*Ach,* I don't know. Each day I have read in the fourth reader. Aunt Carrie is learning to read just from listening to me."

Later, when Martha had read two pages without a mistake, Liesbet Wiens leaned over to whisper: "You don't need my help. How did you learn without a teacher?" Martha smiled to herself. She could not tell Liesbet that she had figured it out herself, and that she and Aunt Carrie had read the entire book.

Liesbet and Annie seemed especially glad to see her; maybe they would become good friends in time. She had not seen the Petkers all winter, except when the boys trundled by on their way to school or Abram rode his brown mare up the road.

Soon the dove-gray skies turned to blue, the snow began to melt, turning the fields into tan-and-white splotches, like the hide of a Guernsey heifer. Then spring marched across the prairies, painting dabs of furry green grass along the ditches and sprinkling them with blue and white daisies.

When Martha stepped outdoors one April morning, she smelled the fresh scent of lilacs.

Fromm huddled near the gate and thumped his tail when she came up to him. He scram-

110

bled to his feet and rubbed his nose against her leg, as though he had missed their happy times together.

Suddenly his ears perked up, and he looked toward the road. Aunt Carrie hurried up the lane, flapping a paper package in her hand. Her merry eyes shone.

"Oh, Martha . . . Martha, I have wonderful news. You will never guess what it is."

Martha stared at her aunt. That look was different from her usual merriment, deeper and less playful.

"You—" Martha gulped a little. "You don't have a boyfriend—"

"*Ach, ja.* And oh, Martha, I'm going to be married!"

"Married? . . . to whom? You said you wouldn't marry Abram—"

"And I won't. Not if he were the last man on earth! But I have worked for Peter Klassen all these months, and I've grown to love him. He needs a wife, and the children need a mother. We plan to be married just before harvest."

"But you can't marry him!" Martha cried. "Abram says if you don't marry him, something awful will happen."

Aunt Carrie placed her hands on her hips. "I love Peter, and I'll be his wife. No wild Abram Petker will frighten me out of it!" She laughed as she tore the paper package open and drew out shiny black sateen material.

"See? This is for my wedding gown. Since Peter asked me to marry him today, I can no longer work for him. It would not be right for us to be together so much." She tucked the material back into the sack and started for the lean-to.

Martha grabbed her sleeve. "Does this mean you will be home all day long until your wedding?"

"*Ja.* There's so much to do. I may even ask you to hem dish towels for me."

When school let out a week later, Martha began stitching neat hems into creamy white flour sacks while Aunt Carrie and mama snipped, sewed, ruffled, and pleated the soft black material into a lovely wedding gown. Martha had never seen anything as elegant as the long full skirt with its tiny tucks and rows of dainty black ribbons and lace.

Soon the wheat fields grew lush, dipping and swelling in the early June breeze. Jake had come home for the wedding.

"There is no more beautiful picture than all that harvest gold," he said as he walked toward the house his first day home.

Finally the Sunday of the wedding arrived. Martha was both sad and happy—sad because her aunt would no longer share her room, and happy because now there would be other young children in the Friesen family.

The congregation gathered as usual, and Elder Wiens preached his long Sunday message. Aunt Carrie, dressed in her shiny black sateen, blushed and squirmed like the older girls at school.

Finally Elder Wiens closed the big German Bible and said solemnly, "A young couple wishes to be united in marriage today. Will Brother Peter Klassen and Sister Carrie Friesen come forward?"

Peter and Aunt Carrie rose from opposite sides of the church and walked toward the front. They stood together before the preacher. Martha was proud of Aunt Carrie; she looked so pretty.

After the marriage vows were spoken and the long blessing said, the couple rose. The preacher shook their hands and said, "Now you may take your seats."

Peter strode back to the men's side, and Aunt Carrie returned to sit among the women. After the benediction, the wedding guests were invited to Peter's home for a lunch of cold ham, rolls, and *pluma moos*.

As the congregation filed out, someone jerked Martha behind the door. "You didn't keep your word, Martha!" Abram Petker leered at her. "Remember what I said. You will be punished for this!"

17
THE HIGHER LAW

THE WHEAT FIELDS WAVED AND BILLOWED, rolling as the Atlantic Ocean had during the weeks they journeyed to America. Harvest was only a few days away, and Jake could hardly wait to move the reaper into the golden fields.

The Friesen house seemed quiet without Aunt Carrie's bubbling laughter and funny Dutch songs. Martha tried to imagine her in Peter Klassen's little square house, diapering Hansie and braiding little Eva's pale hair. The old loneliness had returned, but she tried to ignore it. After all, Aunt Carrie lived less than a mile away.

She had seemed so happy when the two little ones had crawled into her lap after the wedding and wound their arms around her neck. And when Peter Klassen looked at her, there was a beautiful softness in his eyes.

As Martha headed toward the woods, she was aware of the unevenness of her walk. Her limp was growing less all the time, but she knew it would never leave her. Running was hardest of all: her leg wanted to bounce like a ball instead of flying smoothly over the ground.

As she neared the fence, she heard the slow clop of a horse approaching.

"*Hui,* Martha, you look sad today." Abram stared down at her from his horse.

Martha stiffened.

"You should have convinced your aunt to marry me," Abram asserted, his mouth drawing into a hard line.

Martha lowered her eyes. "I tried, but she wouldn't listen."

"You didn't try hard enough."

"She is old enough to make up her own mind," Martha insisted, her voice rising. "She prayed about it, and God—"

"Ha-ha!" He hooted with laughter. "So you believe in a God, do you?"

"Why, yes, Abram. Don't you?"

"If the Mennonites had stayed in Russia, God wouldn't have forgotten them. But here—" He waved his arm at the open spaces. "You will see. This land is cruel!" He swung around and left.

Martha continued on to the woods. She sat

there a long time, gazing at the deep blue sky, now studded with curled clouds that seemed to hang without moving. Then the cloud shapes changed as a sudden gust of wind piled them into thick pillowed forms, rolling and tumbling over each other. Somewhere she heard the scolding *tchak-tchak* of a blue jay and the low howl of a coyote.

She struggled to her feet and limped back to the house. Suddenly the faint smell of smoke rose above the fragrant June air. Martha started. Smoke seemed to be drifting towards her.

She glanced around wildly: the wheat fields east of the barn were raging with flames! She rushed awkwardly into the house screaming.

"Papa . . . Jake. The wheat's on fire!"

Jake and papa jumped up from eating their lunch and rushed out of the house, grabbing milk pails off of the gateposts as they sped toward the well. She seized the first thing she could find in the lean-to—a battered dishpan—and limped out after them.

By this time papa and Jake were flinging their meager bucketfuls of water on the blazing wheat. Martha hobbled across the yard, angry because she could not run. Soon she was staring helplessly at the once-beautiful wheat stalks, shriveled by the fire and fading from black, to gray, to pale wisps of nothing.

"Papa . . . Jake. The wheat's on fire!"

Then she saw papa and Jake slump against the barn, their faces smudged with soot and grime. The fields were almost nothing now, just a gaping black square. Yet the fire swept on to Peter Klassen's wheat farther east, leaving only blackness and ruin.

Martha walked slowly toward papa and Jake. The haggard lines in papa's smoke-stained face made the ache within her swell. He stood with his head bowed and his shoulders sagging. Jake slumped against the barn, his face alive with anger.

"Why, papa?" he raged. "Why did this happen? The wheat almost ready to harvest—like gold to be gleaned from the fields. Now it's gone!"

Papa raised his stricken face. " 'The Lord giveth and the Lord taketh away. Blessed be the name of the Lord,' " he quoted, almost as if the words eased his pain. "He knows what's best, Jacob. We must not question his love."

"No!" Martha staggered toward papa, her fists clenched. "God wouldn't allow this, not if he loves us!"

"That's not for us to say, Martha."

Martha resisted her father's suggestion. Why only papa's and Peter Klassen's wheat fields? she wondered. Why not the rest of the settlement's? Was this the punishment Abram had predicted?

"Well, then, it's Aunt Carrie's fault," she said finally.

Papa looked at her queerly. "What did you say, Martha?"

"I said it's Aunt Carrie's fault for marrying Peter Klassen. Abram Petker said something would happen if she did."

"Now wait a minute!" Jake said, suddenly alert. He came toward her and placed his hands on her shoulders. "Just what all did Abram say to you?"

"He said—" Martha paused, frightened by the tone of Jake's voice. "He said that God was going to punish us, because Aunt Carrie married Peter Klassen rather than him."

A hard look crept into Jake's eyes. "Then maybe it was Abram Petker who set the fire. We'll see about that!" he said as he started across the yard.

Papa shouted after him. "Wait, Jacob! Here comes Carrie. Let's hear what she has to say."

Aunt Carrie scrambled over the blackened stubble, pushing a wheelbarrow with Hansie and Eva huddled inside. Her face was smudged with sooty tears.

"*Ach,* this is terrible!" she cried as she panted into the Friesen yard. "Our beautiful wheat's all gone. Peter says he's sure someone set this fire. He went to the county seat to get the sheriff."

"Sheriff!" Martha gasped. "But—"

Jake swung around angrily. "We know who did it, Aunt Carrie," he said in a raspy voice. "There's no doubt about it."

"But who would do such a foolish thing?" she asked. "We have no enemies. I just can't imagine—"

"Martha says Abram Petker told her something dreadful would happen if you didn't marry him," Jake broke in.

Aunt Carrie's face went white under the sooty stains. "Abram! Why, of course! And to think I laughed at him. I didn't think he would do anything so dreadful, even though he talks foolishly."

"He's full of the devil to do what he did," Jake muttered as he swung around and tromped down the lane. Jake had grown broad and tall and strong. Martha knew he was not afraid of Abram Petker, even though Abram was older.

Papa watched him go, as though he was not quite sure what to do. Then he turned to Aunt Carrie. "Bring the children and come into the house. We will wait until Peter returns."

"What about Jake?" Martha asked, her eyes on his disappearing figure.

"He will bring Abram here. Don't worry about him," papa replied.

Martha took Hansie's grubby hand and led

him into the lean-to. The kitchen was hot, with the familiar fragrance of freshly baked bread still clinging to the air.

Mama bustled about, slicing thick wedges of the soft, warm loaves. She turned to Martha. "Go to the cave and bring back butter and milk."

Martha hobbled out of the kitchen and down the cave's damp, mossy steps. She found the pitcher of cold milk and the stone crock of yellow butter and brought them back into the kitchen. Then mama poured the milk into tin mugs and spread the butter thickly on the warm bread until it oozed over the crusts.

As they ate, Hansie drowsed in Aunt Carrie's lap and Eva quietly traced one finger over the yellow roses on the oilcloth-covered table. Martha's eyes misted. She would never again be sorry her aunt had married.

"We won't be able to pay anything on what we owe this year," papa was saying soberly.

"Neither will we," Aunt Carrie replied. "I'm not sure how we'll manage."

"But the Lord will see us through. There will be other years," papa asserted.

Martha glanced toward the window, distracted by Fromm's insistent barking. Jake was marching up the lane, gripping Abram Petker by the shoulder. They slammed through the gate and came into the house.

121

Everyone stopped talking and eating.

Jake looked at them all, then he nudged Abram. "Go on. Tell them what you did."

Abram moistened his lips with his tongue. "I—did it. I set the fires to both fields, because—" His eyes strayed to Aunt Carrie, and he paused.

The tense silence that followed was broken by the sound of horses' hooves. Minutes later Peter Klassen and Sheriff Weeks entered the house.

Before the sheriff had said much, Abram repeated his confession.

"So," the sheriff finally said, looking at Abram, "you set the fire. You know I must take you to jail."

"Jail!" Abram's glance darted around the room.

"You have committed a crime by destroying property," the sheriff continued. "You Mennonites haven't been here long, but you know you must obey the laws of this land."

Abram nodded. But before he could say anything, papa, who had been fiddling with his empty cup, jumped up. "No! The Bible says we're to be kind to those who hate us. If we let Abram go to jail, we are not doing that."

The sheriff frowned. "You mean you refuse to press charges, Mr. Friesen?"

Papa looked at Martha and Jake.

Jake sighed. "Papa, the sheriff wants to know if you refuse to let Abram go to jail for what he did."

"*Ja,*" papa nodded. "That's what I mean. What about you, Peter?"

Peter was silent for a long time; then he nodded, too. "Brother Friesen is right. We will not press charges."

The sheriff shook his head as if he did not believe what he had heard. Then he turned to Abram.

"Look here, Abram Petker. I have to let you go. But you get off this property right now, and stay off! If I ever catch you crossing this road again, I'll throw you in jail!" Then he nodded good-bye to the others and pushed Abram toward the door.

"Mennonites sure are odd," he said as the lean-to door closed behind them.

18
THE PARABLE

AFTER SUPPER MARTHA WANDERED out to the little graveyard. Seeing Aunt Carrie and the children together had made her feel especially lonely.

Well, at least a busy summer lay ahead, she thought, even if there was no wheat to harvest.

Hearing footsteps, she turned around eagerly: now they could not belong to Abram Petker. Instead, her brother was coming toward her.

"*Na*, Martha, why are you here at the little grave again?"

She lowered her gaze. "Because I need someone to talk to."

"How about talking to me? Brother Franz isn't in that grave. Remember?"

"But I saw them lower that box into the

ground and cover it with clods, Jake."

"Come." Jake took her hand and pulled he to her feet. "Let's go across the road to George Petker's wheat field."

She limped along beside him as they crossed the dusty road and hopped over a ditch onto the Petker's land.

Jake knelt down and touched a clump of wheat with his fingers. The stalks stood strong and golden, ready for the reaper.

"It's like a parable, Martha. In the fall, papa sows the wheat kernel into the ground, and the seed dies. But out of that seed, a new plant shoots up, beautiful and strong. The seed had to die in order for a new plant to grow.

"That's how it was with Jesus," Jake continued, lifting Martha onto his knee. "He died for our sins and was put into a tomb. But the real Jesus didn't stay there. He came out of the grave with a new body, perfect and beautiful. And he said it would be the same with us."

Jake looked into her eyes, cupping his hands around her cheek. "When Baby Franz died, *his body* was placed in the ground. But part of him still lived—*his spirit*. His human body is still in that grave. But the real part of him—the part we love—is with Jesus, alive and happy. . . . Don't you see, Martha?"

As he was talking, Martha had begun to understand. She touched the strong stalks of neat. A seed must die so these new plants would live and flourish—just as Baby Franz now lived with Jesus.

Then she thought about the song their friends had sung as they had carried him to the cemetery. They had sung about going home. Now she knew they were not referring to Russia. They had meant Baby Franz's home with Jesus—a home they would go to someday.

Martha knew her baby brother must be happy there, so it was selfish to wish him back. "Now I understand," she said out loud as she gave Jake a big hug. "But there's one more thing that bothers me. It's not a big problem, I know, Jake. But why do I have to lose all my friends? First, it was Alice, then Baby Franz, and now Aunt Carrie. Sometimes I'm so lonely."

Jake slid her off his knee and helped her up. "Martha, we always have to make new friends and have new experiences. God planned it that way, so we would grow into people who serve others. Maybe the next time someone moves in, you will find another friend. Someone who needs *you*."

"Well, there's always little Eva," Martha replied. "I can play with her every day and help Aunt Carrie when she needs me. I never thought of that."

"Oh, Martha. How I've missed you!"

Jake took her hand, and together they started back toward the house. Already the sun was dipping toward the west. The pink-tinted clouds trailing it were cupped along the horizon, spilling a liquid gold light over the prairies. In the distance a calf bawled, and Fromm barked at a rabbit.

Just then she heard a soft *clop-clop* on the road and saw a gaily painted pony cart pattering toward her. A slender, blonde figure clutched the pony's reins.

"Alice!" Martha shrieked, wobbling toward the cart when it stopped. "Alice Tinsley!"

Alice dropped her reins and leaned over the rig. "Oh, Martha. How I've missed you! Tomorrow is my eleventh birthday, and papa bought me this cart. Can you come over and help me celebrate? Mama says I can come and get you," she added.

Tears filled Martha's eyes. "Alice—" She gulped. "It's so good to have a friend." She could say no more. In those words, she had said it all.